THE FALLING TOWER

MEG MOSEMAN

APOCRYPHILE
PRESS

Apocryphile Press
PO Box 255
Hannacroix, NY 12087
www.apocryphilepress.com

Copyright © 2025 by Meg Moseman
Printed in the United States of America
ISBN 978-1-965646-15-1 | paper
ISBN 978-1-965646-16-8 | ePub

Please join our mailing list at www.apocryphilepress.com/free. We'll keep you up-to- date on all our new releases, and we'll also send you a FREE BOOK. Visit us today!

CONTENTS

1

THE PLACE OF THE LION

Eve Mayhew climbed the steps of Widener Library one October morning, red-and-brown-checked scarf flapping in the wind, heels of her leather boots clicking on the granite, beaded purse swinging.

Mona, typically, had thanked Eve about ten times for agreeing to return the overdue books, each time more pleadingly and ostentatiously than the last. It somehow didn't make Eve any less annoyed with her suitemate. Mona's time management issues, Eve felt, shouldn't be Eve's problem.

Eve could hardly have refused; it wasn't like she had other commitments. But doing the favor broke up her morning, which she'd been planning to spend reading, and it was cold and blustery, and Mona's tap-tapping at the computer all last night in a frantic bid to finish an already-late paper had kept Eve up for hours. How Mona got all those extensions was beyond Eve.

Warmth. Yellow light. Eve passed through the marble entryway, swiped her ID, and went toward the stacks. You were supposed to make poetry out of everything, so Eve reflected that the movement from cold to warmth could make an interesting poem. You couldn't know the warmth without the cold. Could you know joy without sadness, then? The feeling of being full without hunger and thirst? It felt like a very deep question. It was like moving from loneliness to love. She leaned against a marble pillar to catch her breath, beginning to compose a poem in her head (*Loneliness is...*), and pulled out one of the books to see what Mona was reading.

The Place of the Lion. Looked old and battered. She'd never heard of it. She pulled the slip of paper Mona had used as a bookmark out and glanced at it. Her eyes slipped over it twice, uncomprehending, noting only that it was written in Min's tiny, sharp hand, before she realized she couldn't read it because it was in an alphabet she had never seen.

She shrugged, threw the scrap away, and took the books over to the zitty librarian. His "have a nice day" was eager, wide-eyed, and a little creepy. She answered with what she hoped was a discouragingly brief "you too" and walked downstairs to Widener's coffee shop to warm up more thoroughly.

She grimaced at the linoleum, vending machines, and fluorescent lights—didn't Harvard have the money to do better than this? Still, she made herself a sixteen-ounce oolong tea, paid the cashier, and sat down. She regretted coming down here.

At first, she thought the shop was empty except for the cashier, who was reading a magazine on cars. She didn't understand why it took her so long to spot the man in the corner with the rumpled hair and the round glasses. In fact, she could have sworn she'd already glanced at his table and found it empty except for a few crumbs.

He looked up sharply from the book he was reading and met her gaze. Eve managed not to jump, barely. "Good morning!" she said, too chipperly, and looked away.

"Is it?" the man asked in a weird British accent. "Morning, that is—good, I suppose, goes without saying."

"It's 11:30," Eve said, after a glance at her phone. What an artificial way to start a conversation! Stupid, too. Why would *good* go without saying? She'd think the opposite—it was awful out there. Sometimes gray, stormy weather could be exciting, but this wasn't it. Weird, she decided—weird and pretentious. She couldn't figure out how old he was, either—she'd thought a professor, but now he looked about her age. She glanced at his book—something by James Patterson. On the table sat *Paradise Lost*. They were reading that in a couple weeks in her English survey course. Maybe he was a classmate, reading ahead? She hoped not. He almost scared her.

"I know you—good Lady," he said apologetically (she could almost hear the capital *L*), "but awkwardly enough, I can't recall your name."

"Eve," she said. "I'm sorry. I'd better get to class," she lied, since he looked about to speak again.

She walked briskly out the door, into the foyer.

"My dear!" he called, coming after her. He laid a hand lightly on her arm and then jumped back as if she'd shocked him.

She turned unwillingly to face him. His *dear*, was she?

He said, "I've only the right to trouble you any human being has to trouble another—infinite, perhaps, and yet—but I believe —or hope—that it is our duty to receive as well as to give—and that such a one as yourself might condescend..." He said all this quickly enough that she wasn't sure she was hearing it correctly. His abrupt gesticulations were distracting, too. Was he some kind of medieval reenactor, with that *lady* stuff? Then why was he wearing a suit? Or was he actually insane?

Eve nearly turned and walked away without a word. She wanted to, but he looked just normal enough politeness held her back. Besides, what if it was a medical emergency? She supposed she could call someone (though, if that were the case, why on earth didn't he do it himself, or talk to the library staff?). "What do you need?" she asked slowly.

He looked stunned by this response. There was a suggestion of tears in his eyes. He didn't reply for perhaps a whole minute, though a few times he seemed about to speak. Finally, he said, again so hurriedly she could hardly understand him, "Perhaps—of your goodness—the year?"

"2021," Eve said, shaking her head. "I need to get going," she repeated and climbed the stairs rapidly. At the top, she glanced back, and he was nowhere to be found. Still, she said to the clerk at the counter as she showed the contents of her purse to prove she wasn't stealing anything, "There was kind of a weird man downstairs. He seemed—not okay. Round glasses, had *Paradise Lost*."

The woman just nodded and gestured for Eve to take her purse.

As she left the library, a man's voice shouted "PHYLLIS!"— judging by the way it echoed, over a loudspeaker. She froze automatically, and her stomach clenched in dread. But there was no reason to worry. No one at Harvard called her Phyllis; she despised her birth name, and, petty though it seemed, one of the best things about going to college out of state, with strangers, was that *almost no one knew her name was Phyllis*. Intellectually, she knew that, deservedly rare as the name was, she was not the only person who owned it—and that, despite the hint of a British accent in the voice, there was *no* way the library weirdo could know it—but she shuddered.

At that moment, Mona Macintosh saved her muddled, jumbled, hemi-semi-demi-proofread *Faerie Queene* paper, attached it, and hit *send*. Eve had finished hers a week earlier, and it was, in Mona's less-than-charitable opinion, lyrically written but dull as dirt— more or less like Mona's papers from high school. She'd since discovered, with equal parts alarm and delight, that at Harvard they actually cared what you wrote and not just whether you wrote it in complete sentences with the occasional rhetorical flourish. Could Eve really get away with work that simplistic? It made Mona feel embarrassingly proud of her own efforts.

"Except," Mona acknowledged aloud, "I do not struggle enough with my addiction to parallel construction and alliteration and melodrama, whereas Eve writes with a genuine poet's eye, so her lines don't bang and clang, and she doesn't overstate her case just because it makes a nice—*chiasmus*? Is that the word? Whatever. And perhaps I am mistaking simplicity for simple-mindedness. I have no sense of taste and proportion...and I need to take out the garbage. I do declare it smells, and it's my turn."

Instead, of course, she opened a document full of snippets she hoped to use in her writing and added a sentence to a bit of stupid *Scarlet Fangs* fanfic (not stupid by the standards of this particular fandom, probably, *but...*). On no sleep Mona found this critical assessment extraordinarily funny and giggled about it for a good five minutes before forcing herself, if not to take out the garbage, at least to collect some clothes and go into the bathroom to shower.

Weirdly, the bathroom also smelled like garbage. In fact, the stench was even stronger.

Showered and dressed, wet hair in a bun, she tore across campus to her Russian class. The smell had to be on the wind, because it followed her all the way across Harvard Yard into the Barker Center.

She arrived three minutes late, panting, a smudged composition in her hand. Maybe the smell was, somehow, coming from *her*, but that made no sense. She'd just showered. She saw people wrinkling their noses.

"Прошу прощение," *excuse me,* she said as she took her seat and slid the composition across the table.

"Stinks," she whispered cheerfully to her neighbor.

He nodded feelingly.

The smell persisted all through class. It only grew stronger as she returned to the dorm. She checked her shoes several times— no, she hadn't stepped in dog shit.

It did not hit her until she got home that a major character in *The Place of the Lion*—the Williams novel she'd been reading when she decided his books were not only overdue but totally destroying her productivity, such that they *had* to go back to the library, even if it required imposing on Eve, who was so good to help her—had also been followed by an inexplicable stench, which turned out to belong to a pterodactyl-like archetypal being that some commentator thought represented the perverted intellect. The character, Damaris, was an utterly self-obsessed scholar who looked at her studies as a purely intellectual endeavor with no reality or application to everyday life—two sins, if sins they were, that Mona was thoroughly guilty of.

This peculiar parallel between art and life proved even more amusing than relative vs. absolute judgments on the quality of *Scarlet Fangs* fanfic: Mona couldn't even make herself crawl into bed for a nap, she was so absorbed in giggling over its appropriateness. She decided that sleep was less fun than books and so set off for the Harvard Bookstore across the Yard, breathing through her mouth to avoid the skunky stench.

2

THE ADAMIC LANGUAGE

Amy Johnson stepped into the suite after dinner and unpacked her biology textbook, binder, and notebooks onto the desk in their suite's common room. She should have gone to Bible study, but with midterms coming up there was *no way*. "Hi, Eve," she said, poking her head into the bedroom they shared with a cheerful wave.

"Hi," said Eve dully, and Amy saw she had her head in her hand. "So cold out there. And did you see Mona still hasn't taken out the garbage?"

"Eh," said Amy. "It's hard to get around to things sometimes —why don't I get it?"

"Mona never gets around to anything," Eve said, truthfully enough, but with a grating whine in her voice, sitting up, "and you're ten times busier than she is."

"Eh," repeated Amy with a shrug and went to do the deed, because Eve's impending rant sounded depressing. Amy was still frustrated with both of them when she got back, but not so much so she could not ask, "What's your book?"

"Oh," said Eve. "*Milk and Honey,* have you read it? It's an important topic, but the poetry is awful—I don't think I'll finish it. It's probably a little, um, adult for you."

"Aww," Amy said and stifled a grimace. The title sounded so beautiful—but she was a child, was she?

But Eve was probably right. She *wouldn't* want to read something sexy. She remembered the sophomore health class where she'd learned how sex worked, and she'd been—*mortified*. And terrified that somehow Mom would just *know* she *knew* and take her out of school. Now she could laugh about it, a little, to her friends; even back then, she'd wanted to be a *doctor*, and *Mom* wanted her to be a doctor! Mom had to know she knew by now, right?

If, in some secret part of her, knowing the book was sexy made her think it sounded even *more* beautiful—was that bad? "You're such a good reader," she said.

She had just sat down to memorize proteins when Mona, pale, hair almost completely escaped from a bun and coat half-on, burst into the room and slammed the door shut behind her.

"Um," said Mona. "Er. I don't know how to—ok, can someone just look out the window and tell me what they see?" Her voice was too high, and it smelled like she'd stepped in something disgusting.

Amy looked out and saw trees tossing, students hurrying below. "Just the wind," Amy said with sympathetic nervousness. "I guess maybe that's Dillon from chemistry—"

"Okay, thank God," Mona said. "We're not all going to be mauled to death, I'm just going crazy. Not that that's actually news, you know, but...thank you. Let me look again—okay, I don't see it anymore. You win the universe, Amy. So here's a medical mystery for you—" As usual, Mona's babbling went over Amy's head, and Amy felt small and a little stung without quite knowing why.

Then the glass cracked, and a reptilian head with brilliant yellow eyes thrust into the room. Amy shrieked. "A Komodo dragon!" she suggested, though she didn't think they could climb. *A demon*, she heard Mom saying, *didn't I tell you?*

Years of shame and defiance rose up in her. She wanted to

protest. Of *course* it wasn't a demon. Mom saw demonic influence everywhere. She worried Amy was possessed if Amy went out until ten with her public-school friends. Amy was choking back angry tears when her eyesight caught up with her. The thing was flapping *enormous, leathery, bony wings*. Oh, no, no, no, no, *no*. Behind her, Eve was calling the university police and saying something about a wild animal, but that was—that didn't even make sense. Mom had been right all along!

"Sorry," said Mona. The thing darted its head about and glass cracked further. "Not exactly—you go in the bathroom or something," she added, shoving Amy back as Amy squeezed her eyes shut and began to pray—not the Lord's prayer, Mom said that relying on given words was itself an invitation to demonic powers, it was like trying to do magic instead of talking to God. Mona went on, inexplicably unless she was a black magician who'd summoned it somehow, "This thing is my fault, so it's only fair, you know... Besides, you're going to do real good in the world someday, whereas I—"

"In the name of Jesus Christ begone!" Amy wailed, just as their preacher had when Mom had been sure their new house was possessed. She reached out to grab the thing's neck. It was slimy and refused to evaporate. "Pray, Mona, Eve, pray!" she yelled as she tried to keep her grip, terror ripping through her. She heard the preacher saying she was safe, whether she lived or died, as long as she accepted Jesus' promise—but had she? She went to church, she prayed every night before bed, she'd, like, kissed a boy—once —it hadn't been serious—

Then there were the other two. Mona was agnostic—went on about it so much it was weird; she didn't know about Eve, though Eve didn't go to church often. "Please," she said, the crisis giving her courage she could not understand, though she heard Mom in the words the courage formed and hated it. "Both of you—if you haven't accepted Christ, now is the time, how can you deny that this thing—"

"Um," said Mona. "Um..." Her hands joined Amy's around

the thing's neck. Amy sighed in relief as the pressure of the thrashing was halved. She even felt better. "It's dishonest," Mona explained between panicked pants, "and there are, like—three hundred other explanations—not *good* explanations, mind you, but I don't even see how Jesus gets you—to this *thing*—besides, I'm pretty sure I know why—"

"It's a *demon*," Amy screamed as its neck lifted them momentarily off the floor.

"And there aren't demons in every—motherfucking—religion out there—sorry, I wish I could—"

"Let *go* of it, you idiots!" Eve yelled. "Maybe it'll go away!"

And the door swung open. Min, their fourth suitemate, stopped midstream in an angry phone monologue in Mandarin, slapped her phone down on her desk, and said, with quite a different intonation than Amy's, "Christ." She then barked something in a language that didn't sound like Chinese or anything else Amy had ever heard. And the slimy bird-lizard just—wasn't. Amy and Mona reeled. Instinctively, Amy looked at her hands. There was slime on them—for three seconds. Then, through the force of what had to be Min's stronger demonic magic, they were clean. The stench dissipated. And the window glass was uncracked.

"You mean, it was a hallucination?" Eve asked.

"Bastard was right," said Min,

Mona said, "Wow! That was a remarkable experience."

Amy shook her head, feeling panicky, contaminated, and very, very alone.

Eve, meanwhile, gaped. Her mind wouldn't process what had happened at all. Min had sunk into her chair and was texting furiously.

"The glass—" Eve said hesitantly, pleadingly. "It actually happened, didn't it? I mean, we all saw it?"

She'd directed the question to Min, but Amy answered, saying, "Yes! I'm almost sure of it!" Then Amy looked down, almost-black bobbed hair falling in front of her face, and added in a rush, after a deep breath, "That's why you need to accept Jesus' promise—"

"I have," said Eve, curtly. No, she was not going down that road. She'd known Amy was part of a Christian group, but she hadn't realized the other woman would descend to uttering such a cliché. She supposed she hadn't lied—at least, well, she thought she saw God in the majesty of nature, though her time at a Catholic school had given her a positive hatred for organized religion (sappy—hackneyed—shallow—hypocritical). She couldn't stand fundies like Amy. She considered adding that it was none of Amy's business but decided that would be rude.

"It really matters a lot," Amy pressed apologetically, "more than anything."

"I wish I could," said Mona, brightly and even more irritatingly, though at least she was taking the pressure off Eve. "I love Christianity, but mostly as a mythology—maybe ethically too? I mean, I don't buy C.S. Lewis's trilemma at all, you know, that thing where Jesus has to be mad, bad, or God, and he can't be mad or bad because what he said was so brilliant. I think it's entirely possible to be a charlatan or psychotic and still say astonishing things, and, besides, maybe he was just misreported, even I can tell that Biblical criticism was *not* the good CSL's strong point —I think the stress is making me garrulous, if that's how you pronounce that word, it's one of those I've mostly seen in type..."

"Shut. The fuck. Up. All of you," said Min, surfacing at last from her phone. "Number one, Jesus drivel makes me sick to the stomach. Number two, we need to talk. This was one hell of a night."

"You know what that lizard thing was?" Eve asked into the silence.

But Min had to run the conversation now that she had finally deigned to join it. She said, "I am *done* with Project Babel. I want to spill my guts to the *Crimson* and expose them all for the crackpots they evidently aren't." Min gestured irately at the now-unbroken window. "But it's not like anyone told me anything, except for that asshole, and that was a bunch of—New Age *merde*. Gather round, duckies."

"I won't tell anyone," Mona said hurriedly.

Eve had no desire to make any such promise, so she felt a certain triumph when Min said, "I couldn't care less if you do. But they have goons—so be discreet."

"Seriously?" said Mona.

"Yes," said Min.

They settled themselves around the common room: Amy with her knees to her chin in her chair, face pinched, lost in thought; Mona backward in hers, fidgeting and still pale; Min on the beanbag. Eve sat down at her desk, more normally.

"So Project Babel is fringe, right?" Min began. "I figured they were working on AGI, all very secret, but the people involved are at the tops of their fields."

"...AGI?" Eve asked. Why did people always think everyone knew their technical terms? It wasn't like everyone went to a fancy magnet school like Min did.

"Artificial intelligence that's as smart as humans," Mona, who, irritatingly enough, had gone to a public school in Montana, said. "Or smarter. Right? Computer programs that are people, basically, though you'll hear a ton of arguments about if they can *actually* have feelings or souls or whatever. You thought you were developing AGI and you decided to stick with it even if it takes over the world like that one physicist thinks it will?"

"Unlikely," Min said, "but if it comes down to it, I care more about intelligence than humanity. That's beside the point, though."

"Ah," Mona said. "I guess—I almost do too, emotionally, but morally I think people matter just because they're people, not just for what they can do."

"No shit. Everyone normal thinks that. Anyway, the AI people are at the center of it, but they're employing linguists and philosophers and pure mathematicians, and—well, one of the people I've been assigned to work for is this idiot literary scholar I've never heard of, who has as much programming knowledge as you do and keeps asking me to do impossible things that make no sense."

"Which," Mona said, simpering, "you find magical ways of doing things that meet those requirements anyway, even though you snarl at him."

"A bit," Min admitted, with a very slight smile. "But I told you he'd taken to pontificating."

"Yes," Mona said.

"Well, I didn't get into the part where he thinks he's a magician and he's rediscovering this language where words are inherently connected to what they refer to. To which I'm nod-and-smile, and Cole—the other guy I work for; when he wants the impossible, at least he knows what he's asking for—thinks Literature Nitwit is a crackpot. But, then, Cole thinks we're living in a simulation, so..."

"Oh!" Mona said. "That's what my theorists are all excited about being impossible! The language of Adam or whatever, not the simulation. They think *everything* is simulation, though not in a technological sense. They think that because signifiers have no inherent connection to their referents nothing can mean anything fixed and signification is turtles all the way down. Or something like that. It's also about how Platonism is a load of bull. Which it is, as far as anyone knows, but still. What's the language supposed to do?"

Min said, "I never encouraged him to get that far. Which, in retrospect, I should have."

"What did you say—that made the monster go away, I mean?" Eve asked. Min's magician, she thought, wasn't the only one who pontificated.

"Well," Min said, "he told me that even though they were just beginning, they'd found out enough to place us all in danger, and to say the words I just said if 'anything happened.' I suppose I'm glad he did. I'm not sure I want to know what the lizard was, Mona."

Mona launched into a long, confusing explanation about dinosaurs and stenches and the books she'd had Eve return to the library. Supposedly the thing had come to life out of the book. For some reason, Mona found this *funny*. But, at last, she shut up (she liked the sound of her own voice even better than Min did) and said something sensible. "Wait, how did you know to ask *me?*"

"I gave you that snippet of the Language—did I mention it all started with an archaeological discovery in Iran? And it got in your head, and your head took on its power even though you didn't have a fucking clue what it was. That's my best guess."

"Wow," said Mona. "There was something else, too, though—how come you quit your job? What did they do?"

"So," said Min. Eve looked as discouraging as she could; she wanted to finish *Milk and Honey* and forget about the lizard, which, the more she thought about it, had to be an escaped lab animal. Would the authorities be in touch to make them keep quiet? "Literature Nitwit starts asking me *questions*. What do I think counts in life, shit like that. Then he said he sensed a passion in me, waiting to be set free, and when it was the world would crumble before me, and he would love to be there to see it."

"Well, yes," Mona said. "I mean, there *is* a passion in you..."

"How do you think I got into Harvard? That wasn't what he meant. I told him he was making me uncomfortable and asked him to change the subject, and he started talking about how women don't know what they're really feeling, and the next thing I knew he had *pinned me against a wall* and was trying to kiss me. At which point I said I would scream if he didn't let go of me in three seconds, and he was going to have to find himself a different ISEF-winning genius to cater to his whims. He backed off and started going on about losing out on the greatest opportunity mankind has ever known and the dangers of choosing the wrong side, and I just walked out. Then my mother yelled at me for leaving. *For leaving.*"

"Holy crap," Mona said. "I don't know what to say. I'm sorry."

"Not as sorry as I am. That was a year's tuition. But I'm not working with them again."

"Entirely the right decision," Mona said, after a frowning pause. "That seriously sucks."

"Yes, it's important to protect your purity, spiritual and physical," Amy said, reproachfully, but also blushing, almost in a mutter—but, blushing or not, she actually *said* that. Eve was gratified by the look of profound contempt Min gave her.

Eve didn't understand how Min expected any of them to process this right now. She was trying to decide how heartless she would look if she excused herself and subsided into the bedroom without finding something sympathetic to say to Min when the shout came again: "PHYLLIS!"

Amy was stumbling on about witchcraft, Mona about how to bridge gaps between belief systems without losing intellectual integrity. Even though the call sounded close—like, in the *room* close—they seemed unfazed. "You heard that, didn't you?" Eve asked them. When they ignored her, she repeated her question.

Min met her eyes briefly, let out a small huff of something.

"Hear what?" Mona asked. "You mean the guy shouting? It's probably just some drunk dude in the Yard..."

Eve didn't have the heart to explain why she cared. It sounded too stupid, and she was exhausted. She made her excuses, more curtly than she would have otherwise, and lay down in bed. She'd been going to read, but she couldn't even concentrate enough to do that. She pulled the blankets over her head, and plugged in her earbuds to try to drown out Mona's chatter, which, thankfully, Min cut short not too much later, saying, "Shut up, hon. No theory. Kitties. *Ickle* kitties. Kitties with puppy friends. Kitties with mousie friends. *Kitties.*"

Mona and Amy volunteered their favorite sites for cute animals and then, thank God, there was silence except for the occasional squeal.

Even so, Eve didn't fall asleep until well after two in the morning.

3

MIN OR CONSENSUS REALITY

Mona rarely had interesting dreams. They could be *funny*, because, being dreams, they made no sense. They could still, on rare occasion, be utterly terrifying. (Her distinction: if you woke up and were relieved, it was an anxiety dream. It was only a nightmare if you woke up and were still terrified because evil like that can't die.)

Her dreams were, perhaps a tenth of the time, fantastical—people she disliked appeared as red and black lizards, she flew through a house that was actually hell, immortal people used colored magic on each other to the sound of Grieg's "Hall of the Mountain King." Still, they were like fanfic—worse than her bad vampire fanfic, because there was no intellect to organize them into meaning anything to her at all. Even during them, she was half-asleep, bored, and rolling her eyes, as if to say, "Can't you do better, subconscious?" But no, her subconscious could not do better, and she suspected that would spell her doom as a writer.

When, at four-thirty, Mona woke from a dream about climbing down a rope—there was nothing else to it, just climbing down a rope in darkness, knowing she would eventually reach the bottom—she was merely surprised. The dream was more unified, coherent, and tasteful than her dreams tended to be. She almost went back to sleep and forgot about it. Then it struck her that the blue-white light of Min's laptop coming under the door felt *creepy*. Then the room felt creepy too—its darkness, silence, and emptiness. She realized that, even though the dream had seemed like the bored-rolling-your-eyes kind of dream, it was actually an iteration of her nightmare, which was mostly about *doing the wrong thing even though you know it's wrong*. She was supposed to climb *up*. Perhaps this indicated personal development, because she felt merely subliminally creeped out, not shaken with dread to the depths of her being. Then she realized something more important: she'd *read* this dream before she'd had it.

As a matter of fact, it had been in another Charles Williams book, *Descent into Hell*. The main antagonist, a cold, placid military historian, had had this dream nightly. It represented, well, the titular descent into hell, which, Mona realized, was a rather delightfully melodramatic-yet-accurate description of her nightmares. After all, she thought, isn't doing the wrong thing even though you know it's wrong the very essence of sin? The definition of sin, even? Sort of tautological? She pulled up her journal on her phone and made a note of this, and of the fact that, in that reading, not being profoundly horrified was a sign of doom, not development. But, then, the Inklings were, though delightful and insightful and some of her favorite writers, also neurotic as hell.

Of course, the part about Charles Williams books coming true was weirder, and possibly *psychotic* as hell. The smell could be explained. Min's kooky sexual-harassment dude might just be a kook. The dream could be just the power of suggestion, though she'd rarely felt it work that directly and cleanly in her. But Damaris Tighe's pterodactyl of the perverted intellect was—harder. The others had seen it, unless Mona had hallucinated the whole evening. And Min seemed to think it was real.

"Min or consensus reality, Min or consensus reality," Mona muttered. Mona was profoundly and delightedly irritated that her theory professor *actually seemed to believe* that reality was consensus, not, like, you know, *reality*. She'd been going in circles for the past month and a half trying to think of a cogent refutation for that and a lot of other stuff she lumped into what she'd described to her politely reticent teaching fellow as "postmodern blah-blah." Still no luck.

Thinking about postmodernists and pterodactyls, she had a dazzling epiphany: she proudly and defiantly believed in reality outside human consciousness the way other people believed in God; her intellectual convictions were more than game-playing! Even when something seemingly impossible presented itself, she didn't turn into an epistemological relativist! Indeed, she found the appearance of a smelly pterodactyl of the perverted intellect out of a novel on a real, instinctual level *quite a bit more plausible* than epistemological relativism. She surged out of bed to tell Min this.

Min was not there. Her computer was still playing some stupid romcom. Her headphones were sitting on the desk. Her chair was askew. And she was gone.

The door to the bathroom was open, the bathroom was dark, and she wasn't in there.

"Relax," Mona muttered. Probably Min had wandered off for a night walk. A snack. A trip to Cabot Science Library, Min's favorite library, which was open all night.

And yet. Min's black coat was still hanging on the coat rack and her scuffed black patent leather shoes were still by the door. Her movie was still playing. Her pink bunny slippers, on the other hand, which she'd slipped into after Eve made her exit, were nowhere to be seen.

If Min had left of her own free will, she had left without a coat even though it was (Mona checked) below freezing, probably wearing her bunny slippers. Mona remembered that there were goons.

Huh. Mona texted Min, "Hey, where are you? Are you okay?" When the message failed to go through, she considered calling the campus police, but that seemed excessive. Probably this anxiety was excessive in its entirety, because, well, most of Mona's anxieties were excessive. To be precise, the particular type of panic where she thought someone's life was in danger (she'd made a list once) had turned out to be bullshit *every single time*. Mona peeked into Amy and Eve's room. She saw lumps in both beds, and stared a few moments more until she felt sure the lumps were breathing, and not, say pillows. Or corpses.

She went back into her (empty, cold, creepy) bedroom and tried to sleep. When this became obviously impossible, she tried to write more. But not one bit of her writer's journal, not the fanfic or the fragmentary story beginnings or the outtakes, could hold her attention. She considered reading a bit of Chaucer. She considered working ahead in her logic textbook. She considered making another effort to unravel Derrida or refute De Man. None of these activities even sounded possible, let alone appealing. She wished she'd kept the Charles Williams novels. She considered going to Lamont Library, which was also open twenty-four hours and had a room full of recreational reading, but worried that her absence might worry Amy and Eve just as much as Min's absence had worried her.

Just as she decided for the third time *not* to go to Lamont, Eve's yell came through the door: "Get *out* of here or I'm calling the police! Before this morning I'd never seen you in my life."

Mona emerged at once and found Eve staring and gesticulating in outrage—at the air.

"Good!" Eve said. "You need help! It's not even a little bit okay to burst into random college *women*'s dorms—"

"Uh, Eve?" Mona said. "Who are you talking to? Whom, I mean—whatever. Are you on the phone?"

The door of the suite was still closed, but a pale and angry Eve was staring as if someone were talking to her. She glanced over to Mona and said, "What do you mean, who am I talking to? Can't you see this *man*?"

"Uh, no, I can't," Mona said. "Sorry! I don't know what's going on—"

And Eve, already white, grew several shades whiter and

collapsed in a faint. Mona went over to check Eve's pulse and shivered as she walked through a patch of cold air.

When she knelt beside Eve and took her hand (Eve most certainly had a pulse, at least), Mona found she could—barely—make out a human shape. "Er," she said. "Are you a ghost?"

The figure's face—it was wearing round glasses; she could see that much—seemed to be made of patterns in unusually thick dust in moonlight.

"I'm sorry, I can't hear you," Mona said. "I wonder. Maybe we should go outside? I think it really is questionably appropriate—"

"You *do* see him. You *do*!" Eve declared, sitting up. At Eve's return to consciousness, the moonlit shape became translucent but unmistakable. It was still talking. Mona thought she caught an *I'm sorry* and was almost sure he was gesturing toward the door.

"I think it's because I'm touching you," Mona said. "I see a translucent person and I can hear a tiny bit of what he's saying and I think he wants us to go outside—"

"You're all trying to drive me crazy!" Eve announced. "I'm out of here. You go talk to your *boyfriend* somewhere far, *far* away." Eve broke free and stormed into her bedroom. The man disappeared so completely Mona did not quite believe she'd seen him at all. Min, pterodactyls, etc., convinced her she might have.

"I don't know if you're still here," Mona said as evenly as she could. "If you are—could you maybe come with me? I want to talk to you and I really don't want to freak Eve out, and besides—wait!"

An idea came to Mona. She grabbed a pencil from her desk and the nearest sheet of paper, which happened to be a handout on scansion. She searched her mind for the scrap of whatever the fuck it was Min had written for her in that strange alphabet. After all, it had supposedly produced Damaris' pterodactyl; maybe it could make a ghost visible. "Please wait," she repeated pleadingly, as she tried several times to write it out. She wasted a few moments trying to figure out which iteration was correct and then just held out the whole handout. "Pick this up from my hand if you're really there, ok?"

Suddenly, there was, indeed, a man—silvery-haired, perfectly solid, wearing a nubby blue three-piece suit, clasping the paper and staring at her intently. She jumped, shrieked, and let go. He looked at it more closely, snorted a bit, looked hastily at her and away again. He had a sharp, triangular nose, the round glasses she had glimpsed, and he looked familiar. *Very* familiar. Weirdly, impossibly—"Charles Williams!" she announced.

"We've met?" he asked, frowning a bit, neither affirming the name nor denying it.

"Uh," Mona said. Usually she outran embarrassment, or, rather, crippling social anxiety, by saying exactly what was passing through her mind. She had learned through hard experience that the other option was petrified silence, which was usually less pleasant for the other person and almost always less pleasant for *her*. Unfortunately, something about the perhaps-ghostly perhaps-Charles-Williams' intent gaze—and the pterodactyl—and everything else about this day—caused her to miss the window of babble (babel?)-opportunity.

Accordingly, what came out was an incoherent mess. "Er," she said. "Like, your books. I like them! A lot! Well, mostly—at least, if you *are*—I mean—my roommate is missing—and there are goons, supposedly—"

"I am dead, you see," he observed, gesturing toward the door, "and I take it this is, from my perspective, the future? 2021, your friend said?"

"Yes!" Mona said. "I mean—would you like a coat? It's cold out there! You can borrow mine. I don't quite feel comfortable offering you Min's, over there." She darted into her bedroom, seized her coat from the closet, and then slipped on her sandals.

"No, no," said Charles Williams (could it really be?) vaguely at the long, black coat, clearly embarrassed. "I am used to the cold."

"That's all the more reason," Mona said, adding, with a blush, "er, something about bear ye one another's burdens? I can be cold! I really don't mind." Charles Williams had, or, *had* had, strange beliefs about the doctrine (apparently a certain, very specific Catholic doctrine that had something to do with Christ and the Eucharist, or Christ and God-the-Father, or something of that nature) of coinherence—namely, that all people participated in one another's life to a degree that they could take upon themselves others' suffering. Like, people could have headaches or anxiety for one another. If he believed in that, surely he believed in borrowing coats? "Also," she added, "there exist sweatshirts! I guess the coat wouldn't fit you very well, so it could be embarrassing, but."

Looking even more uncomfortable, the man accepted the coat. Its sleeves were too short. Its shoulders were too narrow. Mona returned to her room, grabbed a sweatshirt from her drawer, just barely remembered to grab her purse with her ID card and key, and followed him down the stairs.

4

THE MERCY
DOES NOT FORGET

"So," she said. They came to a stop beside some yew bushes near Strauss, her dorm. "Ghosts exist. This is interesting."

He looked at the mysterious writing and murmured, "So mote it be." The whole Yard shook, even though nothing moved.

"Supposedly that's the Adamic tongue, the True Language from before the Tower of Babel!" Mona said, feeling proud of saying it to someone who would actually know what she was talking about. "Well, we don't actually *know* that, and I would say it's really unlikely, except that, uh..." She gestured at him. "Seeing, um, people who probably aren't alive anymore isn't the only strange thing happening right now. Your books are coming true, and my roommate who gave me this thinks it's because I had played with this writing. Because I was trying to get her to explain cryptographic analysis of unknown alphabets, like someone found this on an archaeological dig and there was decidedly *not* any kind of Rosetta stone, and she'd been talking about it..." She looked at him more closely. "Wait, are you telling me you can read that?"

He outright laughed. Mona giggled a little out of reflex. "You can't?" he asked.

"No," she said and took a deep breath. It *was* cold, sweatshirt or no sweatshirt. She raised her face toward the wind, hoping to numb herself out of the shivers she felt coming on.

"Then it most assuredly is," he said, now alarmingly serious.

Mona almost said something about theorists who thought that was impossible but decided it was not the moment.

Then she thought about saying a lot of other things about Charles Williams. She'd first met his writing in eighth grade, thanks to her weirdest and best Catholic-school religion teacher—the same teacher who'd had them attempt to read the Bible cover-to-cover; and the same teacher who had, to her and her mother's lasting delight—they were a family of feminist agnostics who'd sent her to Catholic school for the supposedly better education—proclaimed that it was not wrong to think of God as a woman. When Mona had waxed eloquent to this teacher about how C.S. Lewis's *God in the Dock* had not only made her affirmatively agnostic instead of passively atheist but also, more impressively, made her forgive Lewis for making Aslan Jesus, he put *The Greater Trumps* in her hand. It was a slow start—witty banter between lovers was mostly *not* Mona's thing, but perilous, numinous, densely and evocatively described magic *was*, and, when Mona finally made it through, she started right back at the beginning and read the book three times in a row.

By the end of high school she'd read all of the novels, some of the nonfiction, and most of the poetry she could get her hands on. She'd written several literature essays on his work, and she was fairly sure the piece on romantic theology had gotten her into Harvard. (Why that thing won an award was a mystery. Mona had started feeling oh-so-clever for observing that romantic theology —Williams' idea that, when one fell in love, one's vision of the beloved was not idealized nonsense but rather the beloved redeemed in the eyes of God—could make sense in non-romantic relationships too or with nonhuman objects like abstract ideas or beauty or, say, *the worlds in books*, but then she'd realized that when you made it less specific you more or less just got the *via affirmativa,* what he called Way of Affirmation of Images, which wasn't even a Williams-specific idea. Then she'd had to make some excuse for why anyone in a Modern Secular Society would care—the best she'd come up with was the damnably generic *it is important to be able to empathize with viewpoints different from one's own* because, alas, *it's sooooo preeettttyyyyyy* didn't cut it.)

She should probably leave—except he was probably lonely—except—the relevant question was where Min was. "So, the suite-mate who gave this to me," she said, forcing herself to speak slowly, and not to shiver, "is missing. She just quit working for the people who gave it to *her.* And she says they have goons. I'm worried."

"Min, you said? That's the Chinese?"

"Er," said Mona. "That's not exactly, uh, polite, but yeah, she's Chinese-American. Remind me to talk to you about racial politics at some less strange point—I mean, if—like, if we see each other again..."

"Apologies. In any event, this—bit of writing—could indeed cause—complexities—in the hands of, ah, ordinary living mortals. And, if I understand you, *has.* Damaris."

Reality shook again, though this time Mona felt almost sure it was only the reality inside her head. Still, she said bravely, "I'm...tolerably Damarislike? I mean, the me-istic court of me is a real place. Are you saying the goddamn smell hasn't gone away?"

"She is standing there in you. It's—not so strange. You're only human."

"And you're?"

"Something more. Something less. Especially now."

"Ah," said Mona, a flash of memory. She had read not only all of his novels and some of his poetry but also a biography and the, er, account of one of his, er, disciples, and it was from this last, embarrassingly enough (and not the Williams poem it quoted) that she said, "Not flesh or fish?"

"Yes," he said gravely, with a penetrating look that truly made her blush.

She did not have the courage to ask if he, in his post-death state, read minds. Because, if he did, she knew way too much about him to, like, actually interact with him as a reasonable human being. Too much about his sexual predilections, to be specific. Charles Williams had been—deeply, sincerely—Christian. He had also believed that enacting ceremonial-magic-informed BDSM rituals with mostly-consenting besotted young women was mutually beneficial and stimulated his creativity.

This still made Mona giggle. A *lot*. In the way that middle schoolers were supposed to giggle, not high schoolers, let alone adults. As far as Mona could tell, by high school you were supposed to have enough experience of your own that you didn't get weird about other people's—either that or you just didn't give a fuck. Literally *or* metaphorically. As it were. "No fucks" was certainly Mona's *ostensible* attitude toward all things sexual.

This was not a thing he had wanted to share with other people. It had come out after his death. If he did *not* read minds, she needed to be discreet. If he did, she needed to get out of this, and *fast*. Mona could think of few things less attractive or even one-would-want-to-be-in-the-same-general-universe as that piece of her attitude toward Charles Williams. Mona concocted a cheerful smile (at least it was hard to *detect* furious blushes in the light of streetlights) and said, "I don't suppose you know how we might start looking for—for my roommate?" She was, apparently, so distracted she had lost her roommate's name.

"Min," Charles Williams supplied.

"Yes, Min!" Mona said. Something was wrong. Anxiety could make her forget remarkable things, but not, she *thought*, anything as remarkable as the name of someone she had been living with for the past month.

"I'm afraid not. Now, if it were your other roommate, Phyllis—"

"She goes by Eve! Phyllis is her deep-dark-secret-birth-name-she-hates. You probably *don't* want to call her that. Come to think of it, though, maybe that's, like, part of why you're *here*—" Oh, fuck. The biography had also detailed at some length his thoroughly reciprocated infatuation with the librarian at the Oxford University Press, whose name happened to be, yes, Phyllis, though he'd called her Celia and other things too. Surely that was something else she shouldn't mention she knew, except that she just *had*.

"It's not a hateful name," he observed, apparently mildly.

"It is in today's world. It sounds like someone's great-grandma," Mona said, with brazen decisiveness. "*Mona*'s not much better, and Mona *was* my great-grandma, but, uh, self-consciousness about being grandma-like is not my favored form of vanity. *Anyway...* Uh. Is there anything I can get you? Or places I can show you? Food? The drugstore has some shitty snacks, there are restaurants..."

"I'd give a lot for a smoke."

Right. Cigarettes. His scintillating conversation had been accompanied by clouds of cigarette smoke. She searched her phone for "cigarettes on Harvard Square" and realized that the place across the street from Widener Library with the tobacconist sign actually *was* a smoke shop and not just preserving the sign for historical reasons. "Ok, I know where we're going. They might ID you, I still can't decide how old you are, like, even within two decades, and I figure they might not be able to either. Let's go."

He nodded, looking a bit wonderingly at her and the ill-fitting coat.

Halfway across the Yard, Mona remembered it was the middle of the night. The drugstore was probably the *only* thing open, and it didn't sell cigarettes—she'd read about that corporate policy, and in theory she applauded it. "Wow," she said, shame at her own stupidity, compounded with the shame of knowing *far too much*, compounded with the shame of talking to *her favorite author*, compounded with the fact that he was *dead*—crashed over her in a wave. "I really am out of it right now—very sorry, I don't think anything is going to be open this late... I'm sorry to drag you this far for nothing. I probably—should let you go—I know I'm not exactly—I don't know if there are places you need to be—I'm sorry—"

"My dear girl," he said, "please believe me—the sound of a human voice means more to me than a cigarette. I do not know how long I will be here, but tell me, Mona—something about this world I am in. This is an American university, I understand... Phyllis—Eve, that is—tells me it is 2021... You are an undergraduate? What subject do you read?"

"English..." Mona said. And her relief at finally having things to say resulted in a hideous avalanche she could not stem. "You know, that's especially embarrassing talking to *you*. I should study science or something, not that I think the humanities have no value, but they're of less immediate practical value, and I am of no value to *them*. If you're going to study something that useless you have to justify it by being really *top-of-the-line*. You would be profoundly horrified to know how ignorant I and almost everyone in my generation is, I don't know a lick of Latin or Greek, I like *fantasy,* and probably 85% of the things we read I wouldn't touch with a ten foot pole spontaneously, but I adore *analyzing* them and pulling them to pieces, whereas the *ideal* is to love them and analyze them only under duress, or as—an overflow of passion—you know, sometimes I think I contain in my person everything that's *wrong* with the study of literature today —and to prove it all, I love theory, but only because it is at once so infuriatingly stupid I *have* to pay attention and try to refute it, and at the same time so clever and convoluted I can't just tell it to fuck off and be done. At least we're past the time when the only thing you could like was depressing realistic stories about how much life sucks, but if you go before that it's all shitty manipulative love poems. Do you have any idea how much I hate love poems, unless—"

And finally, at last, thank whatever god or gods did or didn't exist, shame caught up with her and shut her up: *unless they're by you,* she had almost said. She had some vestigial sense of dignity. And of not flirting with married men, especially married men whose pre-mortem track record suggested they might (at least in some sense) *reciprocate*. "Unless they have some sense of abstraction and—and—and reality and perspective and aren't all about trying to get her to sleep with you," she said lamely. "Sorry," she added unhelpfully. She had stopped walking. "I guess I like some of the Romantics. There was something else, though. There's something *wrong. Really* wrong. We need help, but I forget why. Can we talk about that?"

"Someone is missing. The girl you room with. Min."

"Yes!" Mona said. "How did I forget that? Min—I went out to tell her something, and she was gone, but her shoes and her coat and everything were still there. I texted her—it's, uh, kind of like a telegram only—technology is going to be really hard to explain. But it didn't work, and it should have." Mona started to explain what Min had told them last night, but he cut her short.

"Yes, I heard it all," he said. "I was—almost there. The future is often surprising, but books help me 'come up to speed,' as you would say. Even when I can't see people, I can read their books. By the way, a great deal of what you call fantasy is tremendously beautiful literature."

"Do you know what's going on?" Mona asked.

"On the grand scale, perhaps—only a touch more than you do," he said. "Death teaches humility, if nothing else. But in this matter of Min and the True Language—I would guess that someone has spoken the words of dismissal she used against Damaris' apparitions, but directed them at her true name, her name in That Language. In other words, she has been willed out of existence. How they could have found her true name...that is black magic indeed."

"Where is she, then? Is she just—gone?"

"The Mercy does not forget. But I do not know where she is. Perhaps something like where I am."

"Is there any way to bring her back?"

"Yes," he said. "If *we* knew her true name, I would try. That takes—on the one hand, someone who knows her deeply and well and loves her, or, on the other—it seems—powerful magic. I know—perhaps a bit of Ph—Eve's true name, by grace of the other Phyllis, and I fancy I could guess something of yours. But I do not know Min. Do you?"

"Uh... Like, sort of? But I don't know the language, I stared at the bit Min showed me for hours and couldn't make anything of it."

"Irrelevant. Call out to her."

"Min?" Mona called weakly, then trailed off. Mona took a deep breath, and yelled, as if Min were just out of reach, "Min! Han Min!" She tried to get the accent right. She tried to picture Min (her mind did not want to). She thought about bunny slippers and romcoms juxtaposed with imperious, reserved intelligence. She thought about how Min had been willing to listen to her prattle, with the occasional ironic, often foul-mouthed comment that showed Mona had not lost Min the way she lost most people she prattled at. She thought about Min's single mother in downtown New York, the patches on her jeans, her perpetual white button-down shirts. She thought of Min's single black pants suit that she wore to every formal occasion, and the fact that Min had been tutoring and working as a lab assistant of various kinds since she was fourteen. "Min!" she called one last time.

Charles Williams listened with tilted head for a moment and then shook his head. "Not enough. The echoes were there, but— and you are the one who knows her best, are you not?"

Mona nodded. "I *think* so, at least, I mean, the others are—I guess they have more normal-people social skills and don't have patience with either of us because we *don't*? Like, maybe both of us are on the autism spectrum? Do you even know what that *is*?"

He snorted a bit and said, "Vaguely. The question is how *they* know her true name."

"I can't imagine they know her well at all," Mona said. "She— uh, she obviously didn't think much of the people she worked

with. I didn't get the sense she talked to them much—socially—
though one of them was a little, um..."

"Too much like me," he supplied calmly. "Vision is a two-
edged sword, and—mistaking metaphor for literal reality—or the
reverse—can be, ah—"

Oh, fuck. Maybe he *did* read minds—but words did not fail
Mona as she had feared. "Worse than that, I'd be willing to bet,"
she said. "Not that I *know*, but I did get the impression you were
capable of taking *no* for an answer, regardless of, uh..."

"Regardless," he said.

"Regardless!" Mona said, hearing her own exaggerated enthusiasm with chagrin, but, really, it could be so, so, *so* much worse...
"So they're using black magic to get her name. And we need to
figure out her name in *that* language to get her back."

"Correct," he said.

5
LOVE SONNETS

When Amy's alarm clock went off at six-thirty, Eve moaned and rolled over. Amy was astonished either had slept at all, but she had, though she really, really, really hoped the part where Eve was yelling at thin air was a nightmare. It felt like a nightmare, looking back. "Please, Lord Jesus..." she whispered to herself, but she couldn't feel anything other than fear—the fear that she had, after all, not accepted His promise. She collected her bag of posters and was tiptoeing to the door when Mona, bags under her eyes, still wearing her usual mismatched pajamas (this week a dark blue tee shirt with squirrels over striped yellow pants), grabbed Amy's arm.

"I don't *know*," Mona said, loud, panicked, "but I'm *almost* sure Min has disappeared." She began listing evidence, the volume and pitch of her voice increasing steadily.

"It's okay," Amy said, whispering pointedly and patting Mona's arm. Eve did not like being awakened. "She probably just went off to the library. Didn't want to keep us up."

"But—" Mona said, more quietly. "Eh, never mind. Be ok if I join you for breakfast?"

"No breakfast," Amy said. "Not yet! I have to poster!" It was true, but she also didn't have the energy to handle Mona right now, and alone.

Still, she almost relented when Mona murmured dully, "Right," sounding almost as miserable as she, Amy, felt. "Well, I might as well at least be up too. Seeya later today. Just—do me a favor?"

"Yeah?" Amy said.

"Keep this," Mona said. She shoved a double-spaced essay at Amy, and Amy jumped a little. Amy looked at it more closely—it was Min's, an essay on Shakespeare's Sonnet 118 for freshman Expository Writing class, with a few notes ranging from Mona's usual scribbly writing to completely incomprehensible. "If you see her—maybe give it to her?" Mona said. "I said I'd edit it for her, and I finally got around to it. Probably overdue, but y'know…"

"Sure," Amy said. She slipped it into a folder in her backpack.

"Thanks," Mona said, way too intensely.

"Get some rest," Amy said. "You look exhausted."

Mona saluted. Amy put on her faux-fur lined parka and slipped downstairs. At the bottom of the building, a tall young man with wild, wavy dark hair in a black suit said, "Join me for breakfast?"

Amy's pulse leapt. "I have to go poster!" she reiterated with a bit of a screech in her voice and a totally fake smile.

"Walk with me, then," he said, and caught her elbow. She shuddered and tried to pull free. He kept his grip. He was tallish, muscular but baby-faced, eyes a remarkably bright blue. *Way* too intense. Probably some silly drama student. Goons and black magic came to mind, against Amy's will.

She said as brightly as she could, "What's up?"

"I'm worried," he said, "for Min Han. Chinese girl. You room with her, right?"

"Yes!" Amy said. She almost mentioned what Mona had said about Min being missing. But it was probably fine, and anyway—she didn't want to tell this man *anything*. "It's nice of you to check on her, but she's fine!"

"Odd," he said. "Because she left in a real state yesterday, in the middle of a project she couldn't afford to quit. You're sure?"

"Oh, yes," Amy said, sure only that she must not tell the whole truth. "Tired and stressed, you know, but totally fine!"

"I see," he said. "Where is she? She won't want to speak to me, I challenged her preconceptions yesterday, but it is more important than you understand—"

"Oh, she went to the library," Amy said, her voice rising, though Mona's doubts were beginning to worry her too as she listened to this man—*Literature Nitwit?*

"Which?" he asked, more curtly than he had yet spoken.

Amy barely repressed another shudder. "I don't know," she said, technically truthfully.

"Damn," he said. He let go of her elbow, slammed his foot into the pavement, and repeated, "Damn!"

"What's wrong?" Amy asked unwillingly. But he seemed *so* upset—and like he might reveal something important.

"Only," he said, voice dripping with rage, "that her foolishness and my boldness led her straight into the arms of—you wouldn't understand." He seized Amy's crucifix necklace and hauled Amy so hard forward it broke and she stumbled. He looked at the crucifix and threw it at her. She caught it. "Pray for her, bitch, because that's all that's left to do." He stormed off.

Amy goggled at his departing back and then at the crucifix on the broken chain (her aunt had given it to her for graduation; it was solid silver; Mom would be so upset). She walked slowly toward Annenberg Hall to eat breakfast (it looked like Hogwarts, everyone said! something else she could never tell Mom). Then, with a stupendous effort of will, she remembered she was doing something. She couldn't have breakfast. Postering. She walked to the first kiosk, tore off some other posters to make a space for hers, taped a poster on every side, and continued, forcefully, to Lamont Library.

∾

Eve's alarm went off at nine, and, unhappily but quickly enough, she got dressed in a nice green skirt and set off for Annenberg for breakfast—and then to her poetry workshop. It should have been a good day—they were workshopping her poem, and she thought she'd done well. But everything was off. Her head hurt. She wanted another two hours of sleep—at least. Everyone else had already left.

Everyone but the library creep, that was. Just as the man in the black overcoat had ambushed Amy at the dorm's door, the bespectacled man from the basement of Widener accosted Eve.

However, he didn't stay for long—not even long enough for her to tell him to get away. He merely held out a sheet of paper, which, reflexively, she took, and then darted off *somewhere*.

On it, she found a poem. A weird, old-fashioned, rhyming poem, complete with syntax so convoluted as to be incomprehensible. It was titled "Making Amends to Phillida," and she hadn't the least desire to try to make sense of it. She shoved it into her binder, in case the police had to get involved, and arrived late at her workshop.

Mona, at breakfast, found herself giddy, dazed, and desperately wanting to *talk* to someone. Someone alive, that was, and sensible. A therapist, perhaps, but therapists, despite tending toward epistemological relativism, would draw hasty conclusions from the appearance of flying dinosaurs and dead poets.

Charles Williams, she had discovered as they wandered around Harvard Square, was—intensely—more than almost anything else—a poet; she had known this but it hadn't hit home in all her reading.

Even so, most of their conversation after they had agreed that they had to (somehow) get Min's true name, improbably, had been about her English reading—postmodern theory (he didn't like it either, to put it euphemistically; less euphemistically, he thought it was damnation as a philosophy), love sonnets, and allegory. They'd wound up reciting Shakespeare together.

She poked at scrambled eggs and French toast—usually she had a hearty appetite, but she felt dizzy and ill with excitement and lack of sleep—and tried to decide what to do.

Her scrap of Adamic writing was in her English lit anthology —Charles Williams had, at her request, written something in the language for all three of them to keep them from forgetting Min. She'd given Amy one bit on Min's old essay (she'd scrambled for an explanation—Amy would surely think the real explanation was damnable witchcraft). He was going to give Eve the other.

Which raised interesting questions. In Williams novels, the real *saints* tended toward something like quietism: erasing their wills, celebrating every kind of apparent mischance, and saving the day only as vessels for the divine will acting through them. She would have expected Williams to hesitate before using the Adamic language for the decidedly earthly goal of helping her help a roommate. Which meant—either he had changed his mind about some of that, or the divine will was in accord with hers on this point, or he was not "a real saint." Or, most likely, there was a lot she didn't understand. She wouldn't have asked him to except that she had forgotten Min existed *five times* during their conversation.

Mona was not likely to be in touch with the divine will, which meant, as far as she could tell, that—if she lived in a Williams novel—it fell to her to be more like a *main character*: feisty and proactive. She had planned to spend the three hours before her and Eve's survey course catching up on *Astrophil and Stella*, but she decided her time would be better used researching Project Babel.

She traipsed across campus to Lamont, where you had to swipe in at the entrance, so you didn't have to log into the computers (would make her harder to track; she wouldn't log into email or anything while she was there).

By class time, she had learned that officially Project Babel had nothing to do with either AGI or ancient languages. In fact, it made no public claims whatsoever about what it did. Its prestigious fellows included professors at Harvard and MIT, including (as Min had observed) a nucleus of computer scientists orbited by a collection of unnamed postdocs and grad students from a wide variety of disciplines (into whose numbers, Mona recalled, Min had been inducted prematurely—Harvard students were, Mona believed in spite of cynics both within and without, an uncommonly smart bunch, but there was smart and then there was *smart*. Min was *smart*, with italics and probably other forms of typographical emphasis as yet unknown to humankind). There was also "independent scholar and polymath John Nicholas," who, from the bio, seemed the likeliest candidate for "Literature Nitwit."

These luminaries were, apparently, pushing the frontiers of all domains of human knowledge. Babel existed "at the intersection of the sciences and the humanities, of social science and social justice"; it sought to revolutionize life as humankind knew it. (Why, then, Project Babel? It was like naming your dating site *Oedipus*—presumably they knew how that Bible story went; they had to think they were rewriting it so that the overweening pride paid off instead of calling down divine wrath—but it still wouldn't have been Mona's choice of name.)

She stared and fidgeted her way through a lengthy discussion of marriage norms and courtly love in sixteenth century England. The love sonnet, as she had, so awkwardly, informed Charles Williams, was among her least favorite genres. She didn't even like Shakespeare's, she certainly didn't like Sidney's, and receiving half of the ones she'd read would have made her want a restraining order against their lovelorn authors.

Ordinarily, she would have escaped her doomed efforts to bracket this profoundly unliterary twenty-first century prejudice —perhaps not with a genuine respect for great scholars and poets, but at least with a rant that could turn into an essay. Today, what with sleep deprivation and everything *else*, the lecture was almost literally gibberish to her—her brain refused to make the professor's words into meaning.

In true ghostly fashion, Charles Williams had disappeared at the break of dawn—taking her coat with him. She drifted back to the dorm (maybe *now* she could sleep?) and was about to topple into bed when she realized Min's desk was gone.

She went back out to check, and—yes—there were only three desks in the room: Mona's messy one and Amy and Eve's neat ones. There were no scuff marks on the wood floor—indeed, there was not the slightest indication anything had moved. Not only Min's present but her past had been erased. Impulsively, Mona searched for "Min Han" and "Harvard." A couple of them turned up—it was not an uncommon name—but not the one Mona knew.

"This is the last straw!" Eve emerged from her and Amy's room to say. "What are you all trying to do to me?"

"Wha—you mean the desks? Yeah, I—that's incredibly weird. I have theories, but they sound batshit."

"Of course I mean the desks!" Eve said. "You did this!"

"Trust me, I did *not*. How many people do you think it would take to get a whole desk out of here without scuffing the floor?"

"How should I know? You could have gotten your boyfriend in to help. All I know is it's not here, and it didn't just *disappear*."

"But—I think that's precisely what it did," Mona said. "And he's not my boyfriend, he's—" But Mona did not think Eve was ready to hear about Charles Williams, so she trailed off.

"How stupid do I look?"

"I mean, I was thinking this through last night, and I suppose another possibility is epistemological relativism, we all have our own truths and that," Mona said. "But this situation illustrates precisely why that's ridiculous, at least in a literal interpretation— your beliefs about my mental state, namely that I and maybe Amy somehow got her desk out of here without making a single mark on the floor, are, from my perspective, actually impossible, because I'm me, and I know I didn't, so it really is possible to be wrong—"

Eve was looking at her with profound contempt and rage. Mona had known it wasn't the *right* approach exactly, and clearly it was one of the substantial minority of occasions when *not right exactly* meant *not even in the ballpark*. "I'm sorry," Mona said, "That's—silly. Just do me a favor. Look up a list of past ISEF winners. International Science and Engineering Fair."

"What's that supposed to tell me?" Eve asked.

"Min placed in that twice and won her junior year of high school. And she's no longer listed."

"Why the hell would I believe *you* about that?"

"Ok, then just look for her online somewhere. You won't find her. Look at the registrar's website. She's not listed. Min has disappeared. We're talking magic here. We're talking total erasure."

"Mona, you need help," Eve said. "This is absolutely sick. What are you going to do when she gets back? Unless you killed her? Or she's probably in on it. I don't understand why you all would think something like this is *funny*. I'm not going to take this." Eve pushed past Mona and out the door through which Mona had just entered.

6

MAKING AMENDS
TO PHILLIDA

E ve, shaking, stepped into the crisp October air. At least there was some sun today. She took a few deep breaths to steady herself and then set out to walk around the yard on the brick path outside its wall.

She would not spend one more night with these women. That was the first thing she resolved. She tried to think of anywhere she could stay instead and came up blank. She could, she supposed, get a hotel, but that was a lot of money.

She took out her phone several times—to call Min, to call the police—and each time put it back. She did not trust herself to be rational at all. She didn't know what was going on.

Why did these things happen to *her*? Her roommates were annoying, it was true, but she hadn't thought they were malicious. Against her will, she saw the lizard sticking into the room in her mind's eye. Hallucinogens?

She finally settled on calling CAMHS, the Harvard mental health hotline.

"Hi, this is Sarah," said the too-calm, too-friendly voice on the other line. "Isn't this fall weather something?

Eve let out a screech as she almost ran into a man. Her phone clattered to the asphalt—God, say she hadn't broken it, it was new.

She almost screamed outright when she saw who it was: not just *a* man. *The* man, from the library, who'd given her the poem. Mona's—if not boyfriend, then *something*. He was wearing Mona's *coat*, and it didn't fit him at all. "Phyllis," he said.

"Eve," she corrected him.

"But your birth name is Phyllis," he said.

"How do you *know* that?" she wailed. "I never saw you in my *life*, not before yesterday—"

"I loved someone by that name when I was alive. I would not have been summoned here if you had had any other name." He held out her phone.

"When you were—" she said. After a moment or two, she took the phone from his outstretched hand, and it came to life. It seemed to be okay.

"When I was alive," he repeated, more gently. "Something very strange is happening. Your name helps, but it's not just your name. You must have seen some of the Language, too, before I gave it to you."

"The language—you mean what Min and Mona were going on about?"

"Yes," he said gravely. "It is not meant for living, fallen mortals."

"Who are you?" she asked hopelessly.

"That is an interesting question," he said. "I—have called myself Taliessin, but I am not he, not precisely. I certainly am not Bors, who has passed beyond. That is the man who created me, who Mona thinks I am. I am—that man's voice. The echo of that man's voice. I have—a mind of sorts. I see. I cannot be seen, except..."

"You need help; I'm calling the police," Eve said for what felt like the tenth time over these past two days, but she said it dully.

"They will not see me unless I choose to let them. Mona gave me that power with the bit of language she gave *me*. They will think you are the one seeing things that are not there."

Eve drew breath to scream—which, if he was right, was the worst possible response—and then exhaled slowly. He remained, his eyes fixed on her. "What do you *want*?" she asked finally, weakly.

"Your missing roommate," he said. "Her name."

"Min?" she said.

"Yes, but—her true name. In that tongue. If you call out to her—if you think of her, of who she really is—I will catch echoes of it. We will also ask Amy."

"Yes, and everyone will stare at me and think I'm out of my mind!"

Something grew harder in his look. "You'd rather she were dead than you embarrassed? That is not the Phyllis I know."

She gaped. Of all the ridiculous—"Of course not," she said. "But yelling for her won't help anything. Besides, she's just playing some stupid joke—"

"I'll go away if you do," he observed wryly—and bitterly, she thought. Bitterness was ridiculous. It was entirely, *entirely* natural for her to want him gone, whoever he was.

Regarding that—she didn't know if he was a madman, a hallucination, or, indeed, in on some bizarrely intricate practical joke. There was no reason at all to believe him about *anything*, least of all leaving her alone. But for some reason she did not understand—some yielding politeness that had been drummed into her as a girl, that she could not seem to shake—she said, rather quaveringly, "Min! Where are you, Min?" And she felt for an instant like she was seeing Min in her mind's eye, curt and arrogant and inexplicable, in that hideously strait-laced button-down shirt. She didn't know Min. She didn't like Min. But she saw Min.

The man bowed, thanked her, and—disappeared. *Into thin air.* Shaking, she stood regarding the row of shops on Harvard Square for a minute or two, then returned slowly to the dorm.

❦

Amy came into the suite to discover no one home—except a total stranger at Min's desk. A tall woman with long, golden hair—blonder and even longer than Mona's—in some complex braided bun thing and a low-cut, long, silvery nightgown. Her makeup looked like it had taken *hours*—unless her skin was just that good? "Hello, Amy," she said, smiling. "I hope you're in a better mood than Mona and Eve. Eve was so grumpy, and Mona was up all last night with that creepy man..."

Amy goggled for a few moments. "Hi," she said weakly. "I think—maybe—you have the wrong room? What's your name?" But as she looked at the desk, it was in no way Min's. There was a lava lamp on it, lighting the room in eerie pinks and reds, reflecting off the woman's eyes so they looked reddish too, a different laptop (metallic pink), and a painting on the wall. "Or maybe I have the wrong room?" she asked, realizing as she said it that that couldn't be either, since this woman seemed to know all of them.

"Honey, are you feeling ok?" the woman asked, taking Amy's elbow. Her soft hand made Amy shiver in a way she didn't like—but didn't entirely *not* like either. Amy looked up into her face, trying to understand anything about her, and when she said, "You know me! I'm the same Lillian I've been all year!"—Amy almost believed it.

"No—no, I don't know you," Amy said firmly all the same, but she felt raw and rude and gross saying it. Had this—Lillian—been burning incense? Or did she have some very nice perfume? There was a strange smell. A *good* smell. She searched over her memories, but she couldn't concentrate. She realized too late to sit down that she was about to faint.

She woke up what seemed only a moment later, after some nightmare. It *had* been a nightmare, right? She'd been paralyzed, helpless as something hot closed around her, about to destroy her, and she'd screamed and screamed, and no sound had come out—

and some part of her was not relieved but *disappointed* to wake up, maybe because it was so completely and obviously not her fault, and also because—because—but she didn't want to think about that. She lay in the lower bunk with Lillian's hand on her forehead. She sat up at once, felt dizzy, and lay back down.

"Sweetheart," said Lillian. "You have a high fever. You need to rest."

"No, I have midterms coming up," Amy said breathlessly, almost at random, but she realized at once it was true, even if studying was also completely impossible right now. "I'll fail if I can't—" And she would have subsided back into sleep, or a faint, or *something*, if her phone had not dinged to announce a text message.

She shot to her feet before she could think better of it and dashed past Lillian into the common room, panic joining dread and—whatever it was—from the nightmare. Her phone was on Lillian's desk, not hers—and her backpack and her purse were nowhere to be seen. The lava lamp made her dizzy.

"Amy, honey, you're really not all right," Lillian said, following Amy. "And why are you looking at my phone?"

"It's not yours, it's *mine*," Amy said, unlocking it with a fingerprint to prove it and seeing the text message from Mona on the screen: *For the tenth time, get out if you can, do NOT trust the new suitemate, meet us at Cabot Science Library.* And she tore out of the room with the phone, not even bothering to put on shoes or wondering how she would get back in. Looking at her phone again, she found it was eleven at night. She'd been unconscious for hours?

She called Mona at once, but Lillian was somehow right behind her and took the phone from her hand. "Hi Mona!" Lillian said—sounding exactly, *exactly* like Amy (she hated the sound of her own voice in recordings, but she knew it). Amy grabbed the phone back and yelled, "Help!" and hit the ground as Lillian tackled her. She just barely avoided hitting her head and was trying to wriggle free when a shout rang out across the entire

Yard: "CHARLES WILLIAMS!" It was Mona's voice, high and sharp and panicked. Weirdly, Amy was not entirely sure the words had been *Charles Williams*. They had sounded a bit different. Lillian froze just long enough for Amy to get free, without even her phone, and start pelting toward the Science Center, disregarding the paths and trampling across grass with impunity.

She nearly screamed when someone grabbed her arm, but it wasn't Lillian. It was a man, with rumpled brownish hair—or was it graying? she couldn't tell in this light—and round glasses. He said in a thick British accent, "Keep running. Can't banish the succubus, trying to hold it up." She looked back to see a five-pointed star of golden light in the air. A pentagram! More witchcraft! She ran from it—and from *Lillian*—as hard as she could.

Right outside the entrance to the Cabot Science Library, Mona saw Amy—but with her hair every which way, and without so much as a purse. Shit. She wasn't going to be able to swipe in. For a second, Mona, weak with sleep deprivation, impossibilities upon impossibilities, and now blood loss, thought this was a hopeless situation. She looked pleadingly at Eve, but Eve was pale and shaky and disinclined to speak even six hours and what felt like several hundred attempted explanations later. At least she wasn't accusing Mona of trying to drive her crazy anymore.

When Eve shrugged fractionally, Mona towed her out of the library to greet Amy.

Amy hugged Mona, who noticed a pair of bloody puncture wounds in her neck. Shit. "The demons," Amy moaned.

"Yeah, I, uh—" said Mona.

"Shhh," Eve said.

There were only two or three guards and a student or two scattered throughout the Science Center, and they had to sound very, very strange. "I think there's an empty classroom this way, so you won't need your ID," Mona said cheerfully. "C'mon."

They followed into a large, empty room downstairs.

"They're *demons*," Amy said again. "They *are*. What if she comes after us? I'm scared."

"Yes, Lillian...probably qualifies as a demon," Mona acknowledged. "I think... I think... Just, let's see if I can do any better explaining this time, though no promises. Eve? Amy?"

Eve nodded.

"We need to *pray*," Amy moaned, "only I *can't*, I'm trying right now and my mind just goes blank."

"I'm not sure..." said Eve.

Mona climbed onto a desk and sat in a half-lotus on top of it. "So. First things first. I am not, not, *not* reading any more fiction after this. It seems to come *true*, and that's because of the Language. It had better not be permanent. Fiction is, like, a good forty percent of my reason for being alive. The ghost is my favorite author. More or less. Project Babel is what made Min disappear. And Amy, I think...uh...I am the opposite of anything anyone would call an expert on any of this but, uh, about praying, well, I think aforesaid favorite author would say you need to trust that under the Protection you're protected and not need to, like, feel anything... What's the worst that can happen to you? And if the Will is Done, the Will is the thing that's *supposed to happen*, and even if that's, like, damnation, let alone, like, being a little scared, that's what has to..."

"Who's Min?" asked Amy vaguely, clearly not following a word Mona was saying, thank God. Mona was not sure she was following a word she was saying either, and she was positive that threatening Amy with a damnation she, Mona, did not believe in as anything other than a thought experiment was the polar opposite of comforting. She yanked on her hair, trying to make herself concentrate.

Eve rubbed her eyes, and sank into another desk. She put her head in her arms and did not look up.

"I think Lillian was right about one thing," Mona said. "We need sleep."

"But she'll come *back*," said Amy.

"Yeah, it's kind of a problem," Mona agreed. "But let's stick together. Maybe we can sleep in shifts?"

"Where is he?" asked Eve without looking up. Mona could barely make out what she was saying. "You brought him."

"Probably trying to distract Lillian," said Mona. "I hope he's all right. As a matter of fact, maybe I need to go see—"

"No!" Amy and Eve chorused. Eve's head poked up. They looked at her, like they both, impossibly, were *counting* on her.

"Right," said Mona. "Stick together. Yeah. Uh."

7

THE MOST EMBARRASSING
THING SHE HAD EVER
WRITTEN IN HER LIFE

There was a knock at the door, and then, coming through it, in a familiar British accent, "Mona? Phyllis? Amy?"

Mona sagged with relief. Eve grimaced a little at the *Phyllis* but looked, astonishingly, almost as relieved as Mona felt. Mona leaped up, wrenched open the door, and there he was, looking solid, tired, shaken, and holding Amy's backpack.

"Charles, dear," came Lillian's voice, floating like poisoned attar of rose down the hallway.

Mona remembered the feeling of fangs in her neck—and a number of other, equally intense feelings which had been painful, frightening, and thoroughly delightful—and watched with the blankness of a sleep-deprived blood-deprived zombie as Charles Williams stood in the doorway, until her brain clicked into place. No. *Demon*. Not even *remotely* okay, and here *he* was, her *favorite author*, and not just her favorite author but her favorite author *trying to defend her*, and all she could do was stare like aforementioned sleep-deprived, blood-deprived zombie?

She shoved herself beside him and found herself looking briefly straight into Lillian's deep, red-glinting blue eyes. But Lillian looked so much like an idealized version of her that it was too embarrassing to meet her gaze. She looked down and was caught by Lillian's cleavage next—and that was the last straw. "Fucking. Fuck. Off," she said. But the echo of the words in the hall sounded more like what Min had barked at her pterodactyl, and—miraculously, impossibly—Lillian *was gone.*

"She's *gone*," adumbrated Amy, looking dizzy and relieved and—was that disappointment?

"What?" said Eve. "What did you just say? Was it in—the language you were talking about?"

"Evidently," said Mona.

"Yes," said...Charles? Mr. Williams, as if she were ten? Professor Williams, even though he had never actually been a professor? C.S. Lewis had arranged for him to lecture at Oxford, but he'd never even finished college. Total autodidact. CW, Mona decided at last. His friends had called him that, and while considering him a friend was more than a little presumptuous, *CW* felt less awkward than any of the other options.

"How could you do that?" said Amy. "I was trying and trying—"

"I wrote her," Mona admitted, feeling herself blushing. "She is *easily* the most embarrassing thing I have ever written in my *life*, if you want to get technical, and I've written some pretty embarrassing—I mean, I was trying to write a *vampire novel*. I was *fourteen years old*. And then I was, uh, rereading it, and then I got confused and she was sitting where Min was supposed to sit and... The only difference was in my story her name was Valdina. And, uh, she was supposed to be one of the *good* guys, good after the fashion of a sexy vampire, you know, only..."

"Interesting," said CW. "I was rather under the impression *I* had written her."

"Good?" asked Eve disbelievingly. "When I came in, there was all that blood and—"

"Good," Mona affirmed stubbornly. "Except this one—Lillian—had already basically told me she was going to destroy me body and soul when you came back in, for which return, I repeat, *thank you*... Regardless."

"Regardless," agreed CW.

"Er," said Mona. "Um. Amy, I don't believe you've met my friend—this person, whose name is a matter of some complexity, he and Eve assure me—but, uh, is it all right if we call you...uh... Mr. Williams?" Mona had the strong feeling that Amy would take even less well to the idea of a ghost than Eve had, given her religious beliefs, which was, perhaps, something of an irony, given that Amy might well be the closest CW had to a coreligionist in the room.

"Yes," he said. He looked about to say more but did not.

Amy still looked very confused. "Mona, you wrote that—that —I didn't even know you were a writer."

"After a fashion, mostly hideous fanfic I truly hope will never see the light of day, in *any* sense, regarding which I hope I can break this thing of everything I write coming true on me, because I do not fancy writing only about events that it'd be ok if they happened IRL..."

"Where do you think she went?" Amy asked. Amy shivered, but—was that look on her face *wistful*? Mona was not sure whether she was more horrified that she might be partially responsible for corrupting her fundamentalist suitemate with vampires or that *that* was Amy's idea of an attractive vampire. Had she never read, like, *any literary vampires at all*? Probably not...

"I hope back into the computer file from whence she came," Mona said. "But we need to focus on getting Min back."

"Who's Min?" Amy repeated fuzzily.

"The suitemate Lillian replaced," Mona explained. "I gave you her paper to pass along this morning, if you remember, and I bet the fact that you lost it is why you don't remember her. She was working for this thing called Project Babel."

"Why—" said Amy.

CW thrust Amy's backpack at her. "It was in the trash," he said.

Amy unzipped the backpack, a look of profound relief on her face. "All my flashcards! My wallet! My ID!" she said. "Thank you so much, Mr. Williams!" A broken crucifix necklace slipped out of the pocket of the jeans as Amy looked through and landed on her lap. She flinched and threw it into her backpack. "Mom's gonna kill me! That guy snapped it this morning."

"Do you remember Min now?" said Mona.

At the same time, Eve said, "What guy?"

"He... he... he was asking about Min," Amy answered both of them. Then, with a giggle, she added, "I think he was Literature Nitwit. I don't know what was wrong with me, how could I forget about Literature Nitwit...I mean..."

"I have a strange favor to ask, if I may," said CW. "Amy, call out to Min as if she were just around the corner."

Oh, mouthed Mona, looking at him. Was there some chance he would manage to get Min's true name?

"What, did you see her?" said Amy.

"Suppose I had."

"Min!" Amy yelled, all her habitual friendly enthusiasm in her voice. CW listened intently.

"Thank you," he said gravely, but he shook his head.

Eve watched this and asked, hoping she would not sound as rude as she had earlier today, "Why did you ask us that?"

The man did not seem offended. He said, calmly, "Because it is possible to hear someone's true name—their name in That Tongue, the tongue Project Babel is attempting to unearth—when they call out to someone they really know."

Eve shook her head. Wasn't the thing about true names, like, some superstition in pre-industrial societies? And she still didn't understand what the Adamic language was supposed to be, other than that it let you do magic. She was starting to believe that, at least, but it was hard. She was oddly grateful she had seen *Lillian* drinking Mona's blood—it turned out it was, just barely, less frightening to think the supernatural was intruding on all their lives than to think her suitemates were playing some incomprehensible and deeply malicious trick on her. It made something about the sound of Mona going on and on about all the things Mona went on about comforting and cozy and friendly. Comforting—and astonishing. She did not understand how it was possible to chatter and decide and organize after not one but *two* all-nighters, let alone with reality coming apart at the seams.

The man, whoever he was, looked gaunt and tired as he watched the three of them, but his keen gaze did not reveal what he was thinking. Amy—Amy almost looked the worst off of all of them. She was staring into space, occasionally giggling and—yes—had *tooth marks* in her neck.

For Eve herself, comforting or not, she wanted a good night's sleep—a *real* night's sleep, no strange people intruding into the room, visible or otherwise—before she decided what she actually thought was going on. "Can we head back to the dorm now?" she asked.

Mona looked at "Mr. Williams." He said, "I can't say what might happen next."

Mona looked reluctant, and Amy wasn't paying attention at all as far as Eve could tell, so Eve decided to take matters into her own hands. "I'll go back, at least," she said. She stood and left, ignoring whatever looks she might get. "I think you two should sleep too," she added.

She heard noises of protest, but she did not care. She just barely caught Mona's yelled "Text me when you get there" from down the hall. She shivered as she left the Science Center, though. Her phone said it was after midnight, and she tried to get to bed by ten.

Back in the dorm, she hung her backpack in the closet, changed into pajamas, barely remembered to text Mona that she was safely home, and climbed into her bed. Rather to her own surprise, she was asleep within seconds.

~

"I hope letting her go wasn't a bad idea. I still think we should stick together, but I guess none of us has a clue what's really going on..." Mona was saying as Amy watched her and that man she liked. Amy was trying to figure out how old the man was when it hit her. Mona was *pretty*. Somehow Amy had never noticed this before, probably because Mona didn't brush her long, dark blonde hair very often and her taste in clothing was—*interesting*. Like, baggy tee shirts and jeans with holes, but, like, it wasn't even that strange to see her with her shirt inside out. Amy didn't *think* she was attracted to girls. She couldn't be, right? She felt really sick at the idea, but—then she remembered *Lillian*. With Lillian, there had definitely been—been—well, Amy had been terrified when she realized what had happened, but—"I figured out who the other guy Min mentioned was, he was called Cole Delaunay —" Mona said, and the name jerked Amy to full attention.

"He's the head teaching fellow for CS50!" Amy said, sitting up straight. "I had a section with him but I had to switch to a different time. He's kind of cute. I mean, super, super nerdy, but—"

"You know him? You can find him?" Mona said, staring straight at Amy. With pretty blue eyes that were almost exactly Lillian's blue eyes. What was *wrong* with Amy? She'd never been attracted to women in her *life*, had she? She remembered adoring a few girls in her class when she was little, but that didn't count, did it?

Amy looked down. She said, "Yeah, his office is upstairs. He's probably even still in it, rumor has it he barely sleeps. Would he know where Min is?"

Mona said, "We, uh, need to consider our approach. So we don't end up disappeared too, you know."

"You think he made Min disappear?" Amy said.

"Yes," Mona said, with visibly strained patience. "I mean, the organization he's part of, I don't have any idea about him person-ally. Also—you said you'd met Literature Nitwit. I think his name may be John Nicholas."

"Yes," Amy said, and described the encounter with him as best as she could remember.

"So he still remembers her! Or he did right after she disappeared." Mona said. "And he didn't seem to want her gone... Unfortunately, he's not affiliated with Harvard, so it might be harder to track him down..."

"I didn't like him," said Amy. "Cole seems—actually nice. But don't you think we should sleep first? I'm exhausted and I bet you are too. And, like, that way we can make sure things are ok with Eve, too."

Mona drew breath to protest, then shook her head. "Good call."

8

EVEN THE DESIGNS OF HELL

Mona woke briefly around seven when Amy's alarm went off (Amy was always an early riser, whether she was postering or not), and then at eleven, to the sun shining onto her top bunk. For a few minutes she couldn't think about much else, but she forced herself to check her phone, clamber down, and get dressed.

There was conversation in the common room, and it sounded like Eve had a friend over. Mona peered out the cracked door and —uh-oh. The fourth desk, once Min's, had a laptop on it. At least the person Eve was talking to did not appear to be undead. She was tall and big-boned, with a dark pageboy, a short, artistically shapeless off-white maybe-linen dress, and a large woven purse. She leaned over Eve paging through Eve's binder.

"Mona," she said. "Good morning. Sleeping in, eh?" She laughed.

"Two more-or-less all-nighters in a row are too many, yes," Mona said irritably. "Though I suppose the first one I *thoroughly* brought on myself."

"Not the second?" said Eve.

"I mean—" Mona looked up at Eve. Had she forgotten *everything*?

"Your, ah, stream of lovers is getting a little..." Eve did not finish the sentence, except with a snort and a snicker. "There was *blood* on the floor," Eve said to the roommate.

"She tried to kill me," Mona said. "And—"

"That's why you don't date people who are into that shit," said Eve. Her voice shook a little—she was clearly feeling uncommonly bold. "Now that you're finally up, would you consider taking out the garbage? It's your turn. *Past* your turn."

"Right, sorry!" said Mona, guilty but grateful to have *something* concrete and definite to do. "Thanks for the reminder!"

The other two exchanged expressive looks.

As Mona went for the bag, they kept talking—it seemed, about Eve's poems. "Yeah, you've got the stuff, all right," the other said. "'The graying seagull flock'—priceless. The question is where you submit."

"I've tried a few places..." Eve wavered. "The *Advocate* didn't want..." *The Advocate* was Harvard's student-run literary magazine.

"Screw them," said the other. "Your shit is good. We're talking *Poetry Magazine* good. Tell you a secret. I published there last year."

Mona, hoisting the garbage bag, contemplated this.

Eve had clearly been complaining to the interloper about Mona. Doubtless correctly. Mona was not the easiest suitemate, and she had always had the subliminal sense Eve found her annoying as fuck. Maybe the stung way she was feeling would help her be a *better* suitemate. Besides, she didn't always know where she stood with people, with Eve in particular, and having the definite answer of "not high" felt less stressful than groping anxiety.

This taste of stubborn reality mediated in favor of the roommate's being some random real Harvard student who, while not Min, was not a soul-sucking vampire—and maybe, being a published poet and sympathetic spirit, would be a better companion for Eve than any of the others had managed to be.

There was a problem, though: Mona too had read Eve's poetry. There was, if you were generous, something there. A bleak, *maybe* semi-sincere aesthetic sense. It was terse, heavy free verse—mostly snapshots of garbage or skyscrapers or power lines or something encroaching on nature, portrayed with imagistic detachment apart from the occasional slanted verb, like *encroach* itself—an effect that might have been striking once or twice, but verged on comical when repeated in ten poems out of fourteen. The remaining four had been, maybe, slightly better: convoluted, gnomic meditations on what Mona cynically guessed (you couldn't tell) was an unsuccessful high school relationship. Mona didn't know much about contemporary poetry, but Eve's was as boring as her essays, and not in an edgy, fashionable way, either. The idea that it would find a home in a premier US poetry journal —or that a poet who'd published there would have thought it would—seemed—doubtful, to say the *least*.

Still, you never knew. Mona was most assuredly an arrogant ass. Hyperbolic praise for creative work was—less dangerous than having the blood drained from your body. And less bizarre. Right?

Reluctantly, she acknowledged that it wouldn't be if she were living in a Charles Williams novel, which, due to the strange workings of the Adamic tongue, she wasn't entirely *not*. In Williams' novels, the subtlest nuances of psychology had life-altering metaphysical consequences. In *Descent into Hell*, the anti-hero's fate was sealed when he failed to correct the historical details of someone's costume in a play. But Mona's admiration for CW had nothing to do with *agreeing* with him, and his tendency to, uh, cosmicize the minutiae did not strike Mona as beneficial for the mental health *or*, if the concept even had a meaning, the spiritual life.

She would consult with Amy. She texted Amy to meet for lunch. They could also discuss the approach to take with Cole—it didn't seem like Eve was likely to help much in her current state of mind, and Amy was the only one who knew him even *at all*.

Amy did not feel okay. She felt like she had the time she'd taken an adult dose of allergy meds as a kid—giggly, fuzzy, could not concentrate. Pictures of the demon kept flashing in on her—tall, with its soft, smooth hands, sometimes with claws, sometimes with golden hair in braids, sometimes rippling down free, always with an impossibly beautiful, airbrushed version of Mona's face. She floated through her Life Sciences 1a exam and didn't even notice what answers she wrote—she was too busy imagining "Lillian"... Amy floated through her freshman seminar on philosophy of law, wondering sleepily why she'd chosen that of all topics. As she fished around in her backpack for the correct folder, her hand brushed some kind of metal and static electricity shocked her so hard she yelped aloud, drawing looks. What *was* that? She looked, ignoring the professor at the front, and saw the crucifix on the broken chain.

Horror knifed through the fuzz in her head. She imagined Mom's face when she heard about how the necklace snapped... and the pterodactyl...and then Lillian... She couldn't even imagine what Mom would say about Lillian. Exorcism? Would Mom disown her? Where would she go for break?

Then she imagined *normal* girls. A *normal* girl with a *normal* family wouldn't think it was demons. She wouldn't be terrified. Her mom wouldn't freak out. She would think—she'd think she had a crush on a girl! That was all there was to it! Amy giggled a little. She stood up, gingerly picking up the necklace by its chain —no good anymore anyway—but when even more heads turned to stare at her, she blushed and sat down in the nearest empty desk (not the one with her backpack.)

She'd been about to throw away the crucifix.

That made no sense. She just needed to find a new chain, or a jeweler could fix this one. *She* might be able to fix it with a pair of pliers.

A strong physical instinct in her still wanted to throw the

thing away. She let it sit in front of her on her desk, wondering what the others were thinking. She hoped—*hoped*—they wouldn't notice anything. She almost fake-sneezed, just so they'd think she was throwing away a tissue, not an expensive, nice necklace, or a crucifix. What kind of melodramatic psychodrama would they imagine, seeing her throw away a crucifix? Would they be right? Did she *care*?

After class, on her way back to the desk with her backpack, she nearly dumped the crucifix *again*, without even noticing, but she caught herself just in time and dropped it in her backpack. Instead she wandered off to eat. She had already swiped in at Annenberg, the palatial mahogany freshman dining hall, when she saw Mona's text.

Mona. The name felt like a life preserver.

Mona was part of *both* worlds, horror and excitement. She'd made Lillian *go away*. And she kind of *was* Lillian. Supposedly Lillian was a character in something Mona had written. Amy didn't understand any of this. All she knew was that she had to, *had* to meet Mona.

Mona did not look beautiful or alluring in the slightest when Amy found her. Her hair was a bit greasy and in a falling-apart braid Amy was pretty sure she'd slept with. There were dark circles under her eyes. The eyes were much less blue than Amy had been imagining. Her shirt was not inside-out, but it did have a large coffee stain down one side. She didn't look much better than Amy felt. Amy felt, if anything, more relieved to see this.

"Hey!" Mona said, voice full of false heartiness.

"Hi," Amy said.

They stared at each other awkwardly for a few moments. Amy couldn't tell what Mona was thinking until she realized that *her*, Amy's, shirt was on inside-out. Oh, shoot. This was such a bad day. Such an incredibly, incredibly bad day and she couldn't feel anything other than silly and vaguely aware, on the edge of her consciousness, that she was going to be so, so, so sorry.

"Are you okay?" they asked each other.

They both laughed awkwardly, and Amy said, "Not really. I'm so out of it. I think I failed my life science test, I literally don't even know what I wrote on that sheet of paper and I almost threw away my crucifix and I feel like some fuzzy animal is in my head and I can't think. Mona, what's going on?" She stopped herself from mentioning Lillian, though. She had the fear that if she did, Mona would think she was hitting on Mona.

Mona looked blank and overwhelmed for a split second, then said, "That sounds—stressful and confusing and thoroughly unpleasant. I'm sorry about the test... And, uh, I have only the vaguest and most fantastical ideas about what's going on, and I'm still not sure we're not all somehow crazy, but I think—the short answer is—there's a conspiracy that invented or discovered a language that makes magic possible and at least some of the magic is extremely bad news." Amy watched her say this in her usual clipped, hurried way, and it was typical Mona, but instead of sounding silly and weird it sounded—kind and competent and serious. Amy knew the very idea of magic should sound wrong, but something in that reasonable voice was building a bridge between the part of Amy that shared Mom's fears and the part that was annoyed with them. Mona might, somehow, have a better idea about the unseen than Mom and her pastor did...

Then she saw Mona's British friend—Mr. Williams, was it?—was standing behind her. Where had he come from? Amy had never really paid attention to him till now.

Seeing her watching, he met her eyes sharply. She looked down. It felt electric, and not in a good way. "Something's wrong," he said to both of them. "She's in you, isn't she? Amy."

"Who's *she*?" Mona asked.

"In...me...who?" And, for once, Amy felt not just vaguely doubtful or embarrassed but panicked. She stood up, almost dashed away before her mind caught up with her body, but Mona's friend caught her wrist. His grip was strong—almost crushing.

"Hey, chill," said Mona, reaching hesitantly toward Amy and

then drawing back. She didn't sound anything like Lillian at all, no comforting tenderness. She sounded almost as scared as Amy felt, and also like she had no idea what she was supposed to say.

But Amy glanced up at Mona and felt almost better for it. Awake—at the very least. Something painful was about to happen, though.

"We can't do it all," he said calmly. "Will you reject it?"

"Reject what?" Mona and Amy said together.

"The succubus," he said.

"The *what*?" Amy said. "You said that last night too."

"It's—a kind of demon," Mona said. "Supposedly a misinterpretation of sleep paralysis. Also supposedly, uh, sexy."

"A demon?" Amy felt her voice rising octaves, then fell silent. They were getting looks. But a demon? Supposedly sexual? *In* her? The rage and revulsion that had been hiding under giggles surfaced. She felt the acid rising up in her throat and coughed and swallowed, trying not to throw up on her lunch tray.

But, now that she was frightened, it grew stronger and made her giggle. "How?" she croaked through giggles.

"Uh," said Mona. "Realize how ridiculous it is? That was what I did. Or—like—pray? I guess?"

Amy tried to pray and blacked out. But even as she blacked out, she could tell her body was upright and her mouth was making words. What words, though? It took her a few minutes even to figure that out. There were now tears on her face. She was talking about her mother, how she saw demonic influence everywhere, how she would point out everyone and everything she thought was possessed, how Amy nodded and worried and tried to change the subject, how they had lived in this fear since Dad had died in a wreck when Amy was only five, how Amy was to the point she was almost certain Mom was actually seriously mentally ill but had never yet dared to tell *anyone*, how the very idea of telling anyone filled her with terror, but at the same time also guilt, how she was torn apart by an utterly helpless and hopeless feeling that she had to do something for Mom, help her.

Every word of it, Amy realized in growing horror, was true. And not one word of it would she *ever* have even *dreamt* of breathing to another living soul.

"I feel so alone, and now—" she finished pitifully, but with dignity.

Amy saw how clever this had been of the succubus. It had, with *the very truth itself*, made the others terrified even to bring up the *idea* of a demon, for fear of confusing or terrifying Amy. It would make Amy herself think *she* was crazy if she suspected it.

Dread filled her.

But the Mona's friend Mr. Williams *had not let go of her*. He was watching—calmly, sympathetically—but he had not let go. Did he know? Relief flooded Amy, and in that relief came hope, and in that hope—"In the name of Jesus Christ begone!" she called out. She couldn't tell if she was speaking aloud or in her mind. Then she threw up, this time all over her lunch, and it was gone.

She felt raw, sick, disgusted, unclean. She wanted to cry, but the ease of tears was now a million miles away. What had she *done*? She'd failed that life-sci test. She could almost feel her hand writing gibberish. Her shirt was on inside out. She'd spilled her deepest secret in the middle of a dining hall in sickening, melodramatic detail, calculated to win pity and make her look like a martyr—she wasn't sure how she could live with herself. What if she—what if what had happened to Mom was happening to her, and that was what this meant? What if she was only imagining the demon as a subconscious excuse to do this?

Or what if Mom was dealing with real demons, like this one?

What if they really *were* everywhere?

Mona's friend had sat down beside Mona, directly across from Amy. He still held her wrist, but not so hard. "Good," he said.

She threw up again. Life stretched ahead of her, full of new terror: would she ever be sure of *anything*? *Had* she ever been? "What have I done?" she wailed.

"What do you mean?" Mona said cluelessly, cheerfully. "I mean, maybe you can get them to let you take a retest... Everything is bizarre and stressful right now, I don't think there's anything you can blame yourself for..."

Mr. Williams said, "All things work His will, even the designs of hell."

Amy just looked at them. Did they have no idea what a confidence she had broken? She could still feel her mouth shaping those foreign words—so true and such an outwardly reasonable thing to say and so profoundly alien to everything about her that she had never even said them to herself before. Then Mr. Williams' words registered. They sounded—just off from a Bible verse. She'd even know which on a better day. And he was the one who'd basically said she was possessed. Who'd *accurately* said she was possessed, she was sure—that had not been her subconscious, she *knew* her subconscious, and it had never felt like that, it had never done anything like that to her—who *was* he? He still was resting three fingers on her wrist.

She stared up at him, half-hoping he might understand—if not why she hated her outpouring, then something. Then she remembered he'd also sketched a pentagram in the air.

A greater demon could cast out lesser demons, right? Black magic. She snatched her hand away, and he made no move to recapture it. But the despair settling on her was not complete. She didn't know why. The stirring of hope was almost painful. It was like she was being torn in two.

9
BUCKET LISTS

Mona watched CW and Amy watching each other for what felt like a good minute, before the tension got too thick. "I...I think I missed something," she said apologetically.

"The three of us cast out a demon," CW said. "It could have been much worse."

"But—" Mona said. Hadn't Amy just spent the past twenty minutes explaining why demons were absolutely the last thing anyone should discuss with her as if they were real? But then she'd called out "In the name of Jesus Christ begone." It didn't fit. "I'm confused—" she said. But wait! If *she, Mona* had been the demon, and she'd wanted to throw people off her track, she couldn't have done much better than an intense, heart-wrenching narrative of why it was traumatic to talk about demons. "Oh," she said. But Amy really *did* have a weird fundamentalist family. It wasn't like all that came out of thin air, and it had that strange air of truth... "Uh," Mona added, as diffidently as she could, and as quietly too (she really hoped no one was paying attention). "This is absolutely none of my business, but, if you want to say, uh... Was any of that —you know—true? About your mother?"

"All of it," said Amy, her voice dull and miserable and as sick with guilt as if she'd just admitted to murder. They sat in silence a moment or two more, and Amy added furiously, "Except I would never have said it. Never. Not in a million years. I hadn't even *thought* it that clearly until now. Please don't think either of us is that horrible."

"I—I don't know either of you well enough to have an opinion," Mona said, though she knew this was far too Spock-like. It was, however, the only true thing she could think of to say. "Nothing you've said yet strikes me as horrible."

"She *made* me say it. I wasn't even *there*."

"That—sounds terrifying, yes," Mona said. Remembering a few dilemmas from her own adolescence, which this dwarfed, she added, "I, uh, I also think that being able to talk about things sometimes helps. Like, a *lot*."

Amy laughed a tiny laugh. "Even the designs of hell?" she said sarcastically, directing the question to CW.

He nodded, and said, but wholly without sarcasm, "Yes."

Mona gave them a few moments and then said, "I, uh—if you two don't want to change the subject, that's fine, and—I think if you want to talk more about this somewhere less like the middle of a dining hall you should, like, totally feel free, but —I thought we should maybe figure out what to do about Cole."

"Cole—" Amy said blankly. Then, laughing and natural, she said "Oh, my teaching fellow that was—was maybe involved with your project? I mean, the one that Min left?"

"Project Babel, yes," Mona.

"Yeah! He seemed really nice. I'm surprised he's wrapped up with something so—so evil. He talks about a lot of really interesting things in class sometimes..." Amy smiled, clearly eager to make things seem as normal as she could.

CW slipped away.

They discussed plans for a few minutes in low voices, as Amy sopped up her vomit with a prodigious number of napkins, and then Amy took off with her dishes. They'd settled on a plan to take place at two thirty—Mona took off to Russian class, Amy to shower.

~

Eve sank into her chair. Disrupted sleep or no, malicious suitemates or no (it was just her luck that the fundamentalist Christian was the *normal* one), she was starting to feel utterly thrilled.

Lily had read through all of Eve's hundred and two poems and nodded her serious, curt approval to almost all of them. Eve glowed. Lily smiled wryly at humorous moments, sighed profoundly at the climax of the poem about parting, and magnificently waved her hand and said, "Oh, details," when Eve worried that the contrast between the seagulls' cries and the gross trash on the seashore was too obvious and exaggerated.

She was a little annoyed when Lily picked up Mona's weird boyfriend's poem and read it with apparently equal interest—who even wrote rhyming poetry in the twenty-first century?—but was reassured when she balled it up and threw it in the trash. "What *is* this?" she asked, and grimaced when Eve explained. "I can't stand stalkers," she said. "I knew it couldn't be yours, of course. You'd never write this kind of tripe."

And Eve's heart soared. Unfortunately, right as she was about to ask timidly what distinguished the two, a key turned in the door, and Amy came in, looking stressed and depressed.

Eve had a bad feeling from that moment that she couldn't explain to herself. It wasn't just that Amy looked almost as disheveled as Mona usually looked, or that something about her expression reminded her of Mona's expression a couple nights ago, when she'd rushed in and—Eve couldn't remember exactly what she'd done but it had been really, really awful, it had shown her in her true colors. (She was so glad she'd finally found the courage to open up to Lily about her doubts about Mona's sanity and her frustration with her suitemate, because Lily had been more than sympathetic, and now—maybe—Eve would get published. She might even publish a book.)

But Amy's very presence set her teeth on edge. She was annoyed to be interrupted, but it was more than that, too. Amy reminded her of something she did not like at all.

Amy didn't even do anything at first, just waved tiredly at both of them and went straight into the bathroom. Soon water was running. Weird time of day to shower. Couldn't she wait till this evening? Was she that vain?

But it was worse when she emerged. "Heya," said Lily, gratifyingly uninterested, but now Amy seemed to be in on Mona's conspiracy.

"Hi, Eve. Hi...I don't think we've met?" she said to Lily as if they hadn't been rooming together for more than a month.

Lily met Eve's dark look with sympathetic annoyance.

"Sick of your shit," Lily said. "We didn't know you were in on it till now."

"What?" Amy looked at her, convincingly confused.

Still, that didn't mean anything, did it? "Lily and I have finally talked about it," Eve said, "and we're not going to take any more of this. Either you and Mona stop gaslighting us—it's be funny if it weren't so awful—or we're getting you out of here. You could maybe get expelled. Or at least on medical leave. If you really don't know who Lily is, you need it."

Amy's pulse spiked as Eve threatened her and Mona. She ducked out of the room out of pure instinct.

She *did* know who Lily was, she thought, with—oddly—not the least vestige of doubt as she hurried down the stairs. She knew *exactly* who Lily was. It didn't matter that the last time Amy had seen her she'd been slender, blonde, and blue-eyed. *Lily* was the demon, and she still wasn't gone. She wondered if she should have stayed to try to convince Eve to kick her out, the way Mona and

Mr. Williams had done for her. She didn't think she could at all, though, and she was already almost late for meeting Cole.

She and Mona had settled on a simple plan—just the facts, minus demons or anything they shouldn't know. Min had disappeared, they knew she'd worked with Project Babel, and Mona had seen he did too, and they'd wondered if he had any ideas.

It was a risk. At first, Mona had thought it was too much of a risk—what if they were letting on too much by revealing they hadn't forgotten who Min was? But neither of them liked lying, and neither of them had any cleverer ideas for how to elicit information.

Mona was fidgeting at the fountain in front of the Science Center when Amy arrived at a run. "You ok?" she asked.

"Yeah," Amy said, though she still felt like throwing up. She thought a moment. "I think she's still in our suite."

"Who, Eve? Or Min's new replacement?"

"The, uh... Lillian. I think she *is* Min's new replacement."

"I did sort of wonder... Shit."

"She's calling herself Lily and they're talking about kicking us out and maybe getting us expelled if we—Eve said *gaslighting*, and Lily—Lily looked like she was behind it."

"They were annoyed with me this morning, but I figured it was just... I mean, I'm not *not* annoying... I didn't realize her name was *Lily*. That's—pretty damning. Er, so to speak."

"I agree," Amy said fervently. "But we're already late, if I want to get to my next class..."

Mona followed the still-haggard Amy into the concrete Science Center and up two flights of stairs. They passed a large, waxy-leafed potted plant and arrived at the door of the office marked *Cole Delaunay*.

Amy looked doubtful—indeed, on the verge of losing her nerve. So Mona raised her fist defiantly and knocked.

"Hey?" came a light tenor voice through the door. "Who—" he trailed off discouragingly.

"It's Amy from CS50," said Amy in a voice that managed to sound frightened and defeated despite being pitched to carry through the door.

"Oh! C'mon in! Sorry." He sounded actually warm—though also tired. The man who opened the door was skinny, blond, and almost as rough-looking as the two women—dark circles under the eyes, pallid. He also looked younger than both of them. This being Harvard, he might well be. Maybe he was some prodigy who'd gotten through college when he was twelve. It happened.

"Hi!" Amy said. She looked down and fell silent.

Mona also struggled but managed to say, "So—we're not actually here about CS50 but about our suitemate. Min Han. It —online it looks like you work with her? Uh, worked?"

"Yeah..." A bitter look flashed across his face, followed by an expressionless, closed gaze. "As you may know, confidentiality prevents my discussing most things around Babel. But she's a remarkable engineer, for sure. How's she doing?" Mona noticed that he seemed to remember her. This was—well, it was better than if he hadn't.

"Uh," said Mona, watching his face carefully. "She isn't. I mean, she's missing."

"What?" Cole asked sharply. Mona noticed with hope that his surprise seemed genuine and unpleasant. But he bit off whatever else he'd been going to say.

"We haven't seen her for the past two days," Mona said.

Cole recovered, saying, "Er, I figure you've talked to HUPD? I'm super sorry to hear it, obviously, but I haven't been in touch since she left, I didn't think she'd want—"

Amy and Mona looked at each other, with the same nervous expression—and then, to Mona's horror, Amy started explaining. "We would have except all her stuff disappeared too and—and our other suitemate doesn't even remember she exists, and Mona can't find her online, and a demon took her place."

Cole had gone expressionless again, and after a moment, sat back down at his computer, as if neither were there, switched rapidly through several windows, typing a few things in each.

Just as Mona was drawing breath to ask what was going on, he stood, put a bony arm around both of them, and forcefully ushered them out of the office, locking the door behind him.

"So," he said, quietly and conversationally, as he led them back down the stairs, "given we are all completely and utterly fucked— anything expensive and not too time-consuming on your respective bucket lists? 'Cause it's on me."

Mona and Amy both made incredulous sounds.

"I am so confused," Amy said.

"How about explaining what's going on?" Mona suggested.

Cole laughed humorlessly but said, "Yeah, that's fair." He let go of them and beckoned. They followed—remarkably, to the same empty classroom in the basement where the three of them and CW had gathered the night before.

10

THE LEXICON OF THE SOUL

Cole said something in That Language, adding, "That'll keep everyone else out for a bit. Tell me what you know."

"So. Uh," said Mona nervously. "We have no reason to trust you. Maybe *you're* the one who's going to disappear us."

Cole said, "I'd have thought you'd have realized that *before* you talked about all of that, but, uh—definitely *not*." Mona's eyes involuntarily went to Amy reproachfully and her stomach knotted. Amy's eyes were downcast and had a suggestion of tears in them. She remembered everything else Amy had been through today and, ashamed, looked down herself. They should have gone over their plan in *so* much more detail...

As she did so, Cole said, "I mean, I get it, it's not like you have many options, and it must have taken a hell of a lot of nerve to do anything at all, let alone walk into the lion's den. So I guess—*teee*elldeear is, as I said, that we're fucked. Everyone at a leadership level in Project Babel consented to AI surveillance 24/7, theoretically through our cell phones, but almost certainly actually in any way the AI can think of, and they're a damn good hacker. I did everything I could to throw dust in their eyes, but—we have an hour and a half, tops till all my colleagues know exactly what happened. Then we're out of luck."

"...teal dear?" Mona repeated, too stunned to absorb any other part of what he was saying.

"Too long, didn't read—poorly chosen internet slang," Cole explained with a grimace.

"Oh, *tldr*," Mona said. "Sorry!"

"What are they going to do?" Amy said, sounding absolutely sick.

"Officially? Sue my sorry ass, try to get me in prison, and get you two to sign non-disclosure agreements for a significant sum of money. Unofficially, uh, I have absolutely *no* reason to believe that what happened to Min wouldn't happen to you too. I'm too valuable to erase, a good two thirds of the work in Project Babel is mine, and they wouldn't risk taking it with me, but killing me wouldn't be hard, and goddamn Nicholas..."

"What did happen to Min?" Amy asked. "Do you know?"

"She doesn't exist," he said.

"Why can you remember her, then?" Mona asked.

"I honestly have no clue. Usually there are residual memories of who or whatever it is for a short period... I don't suppose you know how you can."

"Uh..." It was Mona's turn to be tempted to reveal something —in this case, the small bit of the Language CW had given her (and given her to plant on both other suitemates). "Maybe we know her better?" Mona said lamely.

"Maybe," Cole said.

"Wait," Mona said. "You said they'd try to put you in prison? What did *you* do?"

Cole froze, gritted his teeth, and took a deep breath. He said, "I know you have absolutely no reason to trust me, but—they've erased, you know, objects—regarding which, it's almost impossible to know if you've succeeded, because it stops existing both backward and forward and you only remember it for a minute or two, but if you formulate it correctly you can remember that you erased *something* and make educated guesses from the surroundings about *what*. I should be clear. By *they* I mean the AI, who uses gender-neutral pronouns, not my collaborators, who have very little control over any of this at this point."

"So there *is* AI, not just magic..." Mona said.

"Yes," Cole said. "Despite what some of our more, ah, eccentric colleagues believe, there is no magic, in the sense you mean, either. It just all *looks* like magic."

"Then how..." Mona began.

"How do I put this," Cole said. "Reality is—traditionally understood as matter, which, if you think about it, is a pretty incoherent concept. I find it more useful to think of reality as information, something like a computer program. I like even better thinking of it *as an AI*, in that it has the means to modify itself, directly or indirectly. Babel has found—a more direct method. Think of it as—we have the programming language this world was written in, now. And we can use it to hack reality."

"But—" Amy and Mona both said.

Cole ignored them and went on, "So—like, a couple weeks ago I was almost positive from looking the logs that they erased a person. Another intern, I think. I mentioned this to my colleagues and the board. Fuckers basically said, 'Shrug, no idea what you're talking about,' and I said, 'I'm gonna add some safeguards,' and they were like, 'That's not what we pay you to do, dude, the model is perfect and if you fuck it up you're gone' and I decided if this ever happened again, I'd open-source everything. Which had been my druthers from the start. This is going to revolutionize the world, and we all have a right to it. But *I* didn't have the text sample, and I thought this was better than giving it to some government agency that would sit on it and use it for warfare and nothing else... So I did. It is—more than slightly illegal. Either of you use GitHub?"

"What's GitHub?" said Mona.

"Where a lot of people and organizations host the code for their software," said Cole. He proceeded to tell them where they could find the sum total of Project Babel's work, but Mona had just remembered something. CW had said Min might be some-where like he, CW, was. Chances were she and Amy would be there too soon. But he hadn't known Min's true name, so he couldn't find her. Would it be the same with Mona and Amy? Mona thought she knew *his* name—she'd summoned him with it once before. "Charles Williams!" she called out.

It was not remotely an unusual name. There was no reason Cole should raise his eyebrows and say "...Inklings fan?"—correctly identifying the name as belonging to one of C.S. Lewis's good friends and fellow Inklings (their writing group). But he did say that, and went on, "What does Charles Williams have to do with any—"

At once, Charles Williams was standing in the room in that diffidently regal way of his.

"*Oh*," said Cole. Mona laughed aloud at the expression on his face.

Amy looked lost again, but Mona still had precisely no desire to explain that "Mr. Williams" was (sort of) a deceased poet.

"More things on heaven and earth..." murmured CW, nodding at Cole. "I don't believe we've met?"

"Hi," said Cole. "I—I really don't know what to say. Except I have an uncle who likes your novels. And—I'd wondered if maybe the dead were preserved in the simulation's memory, but seeing proof is a little—anyway." Indeed, Cole looked the most disturbed Mona had yet seen him, despite the fact that (if he were to be believed) he had just betrayed the trust of his organization, was about to see his two companions erased, and doomed himself to a prison sentence or death.

"Regardless," said CW. "You are—I can't quite see it—associ-ated with this conspiracy surrounding the Adamic Tongue?"

"That's not—I wouldn't call it—I guess you *would* think—" Cole spluttered.

"Not *think*," said CW. "Know. Know, as I know you and my hand before my face and the Omnipotence within and around.

Don't fear for Amy and Mona. I can protect them; I know their names. You, on the other hand—"

"Have you been listening in on us?" Cole asked. "I'm genuinely curious—because that should be literally impossible."

CW looked a little awkward. "I read minds," he admitted, with just the slightest apologetic glance at Mona. "The mixed blessings of the ghostly state."

If she hadn't been likely to be erased in the next half hour, or erased except for CW's protection, whatever *that* involved, Mona would have been profoundly embarrassed. Now she just laughed, a hint defiantly (served him right) and a hint apologetically (the mixed blessings of relative fame, having your creepily adorable adulterous semi-sort-of love letters *published for the whole world,* including not only shocked traditionalists who would condemn you—or attack the woman—forever after but also *awkward, lonely adolescent girls* who wouldn't accept that rules like "mind your own business" extended beyond the grave).

Regardless.

"Regardless," CW said, "I have one thing to ask of *you.*"

"Uh?" said Cole.

"Call out to Min, as if she were here. As if she were just around the corner, because in one sense she surely is."

"That's not going to help," Cole said, and Mona's heart sank. If anyone knew, it would be Cole.

"The Mercy does not forget," CW said, as he had to Mona on that long strange walk in the wee hours.

"I very specifically and deliberately left human names *out* of the human-readable lexicon."

"But not the lexicon of the soul. Call out to her, before it's too late."

"Why?" Cole said.

"Because you care about her. More than any of the others I've met, probably more than any other human being alive. I have been traveling, and I include in that statement her mother, her father, whom she has never met, and her teachers. Min has always been alone in the world, to a degree perhaps that even the rest of us in this room will not fully appreciate. Call out to her."

"She's one hell of an engineer, but that's not—I mean, if there's some way it could help—oh, fuck it, Min!" he yelled. After that cry, something changed in his expression, and his next yell was almost a scream. It echoed. "Min! Min!"

CW nodded, a sharp, almost birdlike motion. He called out—something, not exactly "Min," but something that sounded more like *Min* than *Min*, and followed by more of what was clearly—to Mona's ear—That Language.

There was another feeling like an earthquake.

A garbled, strange voice, as if on a bad telephone connection, said "Cole!" from behind them, and—they all turned—Min stood there, white button-down shirt spotless, a look on her face that was indecipherable but terrifying. "What the fuck..." she said, now more clearly audible.

"Min!" Mona cried.

Cole was pale, his eyes wide. "Thank God," he said, "but this is several different kinds of impossible."

"God," Min echoed.

"...Are you okay?" Mona tried, knowing it was grossly inadequate and possibly actively harmful, when the general stunned silence became too much for her.

Min's eyebrows raised fractionally and briefly. She took a deep breath, then said, "I appear to have solved the universe."

"What?" various of them said.

"That's what our AI did," Min said to Cole, "more or less, right? In the abominable brute-force way of an AI, of course. It wasn't supposed to be possible for the human intellect. And I don't suppose I am precisely human right now."

"Er, can you explain a little more?" Mona said, when, for the second time, the silence stretched stubborn and itchy.

"It's only one of many," CW said. "Reality goes down—perhaps every fork, certainly many of them..."

"No shit," Min agreed. "This universe is also spaghetti written by an overenthusiastic three-year-old. But I solved it." This time, she did not need prompting to continue, after a brief frowning pause, "It started as algorithm puzzles—like something you'd do to practice for an interview. And they got harder and harder— harder than any problems I've ever seen. At some point I realized I was solving longstanding mathematical dilemmas. I almost gave up then—but, uh. For some reason I thought there was an inter- viewer. Cole, for a while I thought you were the interviewer. Reliving my technicals with Project Babel." She snorted gently.

"The flying spaghetti monster," Mona couldn't resist squeaking out nervously (some group of atheist smartasses had formed a cult of the flying spaghetti monster), but she regretted it at once, and not just because the joke was only half-formed.

"Yeah," Min said, despite Mona's regret. She actually laughed for a few moments—longer than she usually did at Mona's jokes. "Pretty much. Not that I actually saw anyone. I was stuck in a little cubicle with some kind of—well, a computer with power like nothing I've ever seen. I thought—I'd lose the opportunity and possibly, er, stop existing if I didn't solve it, which turned out to be—sort of a peculiar joke. But then it turned out I had written a set of programs describing the universe. The interviewer was amused. Flashed a bunch of medals on the screen. And then I thought you might want to know if you hadn't gotten there already, Cole, so I tried to find you. I—guess I succeeded."

"Do you still have it?" Mona asked. "The solution, or whatever?"

"Maybe," she said. "I'm honestly not sure now."

"Is it the language?" Mona asked.

"Yes. And the grammar and logic from which it is derived."

"Shit," Mona said. She looked at Cole to see how he was taking it.

Cole, seeing Mona's eyes, shook his head and shrugged.

"I suppose you don't believe me," Min said to Cole. "I wouldn't have believed you if you'd come to me with that and nothing concrete to show for it."

Cole made a sound halfway between a sigh and a laugh, and he said, wild-eyed, "I'm a lot less sure about anything than I would be if you hadn't come back. You know, when I interviewed you, I expected you to get maybe a fifth of the way through the problems but you were so, uh, intent I just wanted to see how far you'd get, and goddamn if you didn't get further than I did, and in half the time. Curious—what is, ah, your impression of, uh, how you were invited to the, uh, job interview? The, uh, cosmic one, not mine."

Min laughed again, a longer laugh still. "You'd think I would have asked that question, wouldn't you? No wonder they laughed at me. The interviewer, I mean. I—don't know, but if I had to guess—" She tilted her head to one side. "Oh, Babel tried to get rid of me." She made a face. "Fuck them. Sorry, Cole, I know you didn't know. I don't think Nicholas even knew."

For the first time in a long time, Amy spoke up. She said, "I saw Nicholas. If that was Literature Nitwit. He—asked if you were okay. I didn't think I should tell him anything, and he got really mad and threw my crucifix at me and stormed off."

Min smiled a bit. "Yes, John Nicholas is Literature Nitwit."

Cole let out a bark of a laugh. Min smiled a bit more. Then the smile left her face. "Wait, you turned on them."

"Yeah," Cole said uncomfortably. "There was an intern they erased before you, you know, and I was like—if this happens again —also, Amy and Mona are in for it any moment—"

"And you—the whole fucking lexicon and the pronunciation guide and the model they used to develop it are now available for free on the internet?" she asked him. She looked more disturbed than Mona had ever seen her.

"Yeah, in like two thousand different blogs, Twitters, and GitHubs," Cole said, grinning. "Someone's going to notice and screenshot it before it gets taken down."

11

POETRY MAGAZINE

Min stared at Cole's pale, insouciant teenager's face and tried to decide if he was the revolutionary populist world-saving genius he thought he was or just out of his mind. She was leaning toward the latter interpretation. "You know that anyone who gets that can make fucking anything happen they decide to for the hell of it?" she asked. "Mona got only the 'let it be so' bit and she brought a literal flying dinosaur through our window because she'd read about it in a *book*."

"Counting on it," Cole said with a shrug. "Otherwise how will they know it's not just some crackpot? And *so mote it be* is the most powerful single phrase we've found. They're not all *that* dangerous." She noted that he did not ask *how* Mona had gotten that, or seem particularly disturbed that she had.

"Cole!" Min said. "Have you ever met *humans*? They'll completely fuck up everything."

"Worse than Babel?" Cole asked. "I mean, yes, right now we have some semblance of ethical guidelines, or I *thought* we did, but I mean in the long run. Do we really want this to be in the hands of a few corporate elites—or a few government elites? And it's not like I just dropped it, I explained everything as best as I could, and I added lots of warnings—"

"Because *everyone always reads the instructions*," Min said.

"Maybe Babel will be able to squash it?" said Amy hopefully. She looked uncertain. Min stared at her hard, for a second.

Unfortunately, she was probably right. Min said, "They'll erase everyone who saw it." There had been a time Min would not have considered that particularly a cause for regret, but that had changed. Min couldn't say she *liked* people, but—having *solved* them, she did not like the idea of obliterating them. No, she did not, not at *all*.

Cole said, "I guess we got Min back, maybe we can—organize a way to get more people back...or it'd be even better if we could just kill the AI..." and then his face fell. "Shit," he said.

"You *think*?" Min said. "You *really* thought this through, didn't you?"

"He did it for your sake," said the man who'd talked about alternate universes. She hadn't paid any attention to him until now, but he was staring at her. Who was he? There was something *very* strange about him.

"I hope not. That's even worse," Min said. "Who are you?"

"I am—the voice of a dead third-rate Christian poet Mona loves, doing what I can before—I am called away—to find the rest of me."

"You wrote the pterodactyl, didn't you?" Min asked, putting a few memories together.

"Yes," he admitted.

"I mean, your poetry wasn't exactly of its time, and I personally don't connect as well with Taliessin as I do with the novels, but that doesn't mean—" Mona said. "I feel like the literary canon is mostly arbitrary fetishizing groupthink, and regarding me, I mean, you're talking to someone who unironically reads *Scarlet Fangs*..."

Cole gnawed his lip. He said, "We need a plan."

Min almost retorted sharply, but there was another earthquake, and the two of them were left alone together.

"Fuck," they said—together.

"Okay," said Min, after they'd stared at the places that had just held Amy and Mona for a moment or two. "You're right. Priority number one is to get rid of that *damn* AI. It's doing the erasure, right? You said a second ago the humans aren't getting the names of other humans..."

"Correct. The names should be thoroughly obfuscated. But Babel *shouldn't* even be able to use them, but then they did, twice, and everyone was fine with it..." Cole grimaced. "Goes to show you can't be too sure of anything. I don't want everyone's names. I don't think anyone should have everyone's names..."

There was a pounding at the door. "Goons," they chorused. Cole added, "They should be locked out for a bit still, unless..."

"We're pretty fucked, aren't we," Min said.

"Yes."

"I'm glad to be back in spite of everything," Min said. She looked at Cole. "Nicholas said there was a passion in me. That's how he started. And Mona agrees."

"Huh?" said Cole. "Wait, are you—"

"Yes," said Min.

"Huh," said Cole. "It's pretty inappropriate, given I'm your supervisor—"

"We are about to be killed by goons, leaving this damnable world in the hands of my adorably stupid suitemates and a dead poet. I think you can bend a rule and kiss me. It will be the second time, disregarding John Nicholas, and the first time it was even remotely a good idea."

Eve was having a hard time focusing on her French composition. She didn't see how it mattered when she might get published in *Poetry Magazine.* Lily had even hinted she might have connections. Excitement was making her brain fizzy and fuzzy.

She hated the prompts for these compositions too. They were always so personal and childish, and she didn't like the preceptor either—hyper-feminine, pretentious, and clearly someone who wanted to be anywhere other than teaching introductory French to freshmen. Why should she feel insulted for having to deal with freshmen—one of whom was a world-class poet, if Lily was to be believed?

To make matters worse, Lily was lazily surfing the internet. She'd tested out of her foreign language requirement and a bunch of other classes, so her course load this semester was light. Eve finally threw her unfinished composition in the trash and went over to hover over Lily's shoulder.

Lily, it turned out, was reading an essay Eve had written that had won a regional award, about the experience of hiking near the Great Lakes. Eve herself felt a little embarrassed by it—it was so naive and unsubtle in expressing her love of nature. But Lily shot her an amused smile, gave her a thumbs-up and said, "You've really got the stuff, I'm not kidding."

Just as she said this, there was another—was it an earthquake? Did Boston get earthquakes? And—Lily was gone. Completely and utterly gone.

Eve felt—for a moment—alone and raw and weirdly relieved. Then she looked at the desk. A different laptop was sitting on it, it was a complete mess, and under it was a pair of pink bunny slippers. Lily's slippers were off-white. She would never wear something that juvenile.

On the desk was a name tag necklace from some orientation or other. The name tag read "Min Han."

"Min..." Eve murmured. And it was as if she had double vision. She could remember rooming with Lily this first month—and rooming with Min. The memories with Min were—frightening, not just because some of them were impossible, but because of the amount of loneliness in them. She'd hated her roommates, she realized, all three of them. Not just a little. She didn't hate Lily, she didn't think—in fact, she'd never met anyone who seemed to *get* it the way Lily did. But her memory of Lily was fading.

The first time she meets someone who likes her—that she likes—who actually appreciates her art—and it's fake. A complete and utter lie. She *knew* Lily was a lie, now. She couldn't even summon the particulars of Lily's face to her mind. And, what's worse, the rest of it was not a lie. The dinosaur thing—the vampire—the goons—Min's disappearance—but why did she think Min had disappeared? Min's desk was right here, with her shit strewn all over it. Eve—Eve even kind of remembered having *seen* Min these past few days. Min had been even grimmer and more aloof than usual after quitting with that sexual harassment incident. She had snapped at everyone, even precious, smarmy Mona, who could usually get away with anything.

Eve swallowed a small moan. The Min memories were coming forward, the others—which she could not even define anymore—fading back. She was trying to remember if there was anything more to her ideas about her poetry—she'd had the sudden, enthusiastic, and inexplicable idea she should submit to *Poetry Magazine*. She cringed to think what any of the other students in her workshop would say if she mentioned that idea. She almost felt like someone else had suggested it, though.

She reached into the garbage, where she remembered throwing away her composition, though she shied away from thinking about why she'd done it. Too embarrassing—or too something. Regardless, she needed to finish it and turn it in. Her hand also encountered another ball of paper, which she opened to discover the rhyming poem: "Making Amends to Phillida." She glanced through it. It was almost indecipherable. The final couplet was more than *almost* indecipherable. It was in a foreign language. As she saw it, her memories shifted and realigned once more. She remembered all three things—having never known Min, having spent all the month with Min, and having had Min disappear and be replaced by Lily. Min's disappearance seemed *more* real than either of the other memories. In the world where Min had disappeared, the ending couplet was written in a language that let you do magic.

She could find *no* rational explanation. The creeping suspicion that Mona and the others were trying to *make* her crazy, or think she was crazy, appeared again, like a gnawing pain, but she dismissed it. She'd seen that flying lizard with her own eyes.

If she threw it away, what would she think? She'd think she lived in a single universe, with a single stream of memories, and they would be memories of Min and Mona and Amy, all of whom she could hardly stand. Min and Mona and Amy—and no Lily. Did she want to remember Lily? She did; she delayed, pressing the paper as flat and smooth as she could, then folding it into a neat square. She almost slipped it into her binder, but then she imagined again what her classmates would say about the whole poetry fiasco. She crumpled it up and flung it into the trash again. She would forget. If that was the word. She didn't want to live in three universes at once. Who *would*?

There was a sinking feeling in her stomach as she started working on her composition again, but the writing proceeded smoothly, and she finished with time for an autumn walk.

Min and Cole were kissing when the doors burst open. There were no goons, but John Nicholas, so-called "Literature Nitwit," stood there with something like a billowing, black, red-eyed shadow behind him.

Cole disengaged himself from Min at once and started blushing. Min, however, turned deliberately and faced Nicholas.

"Oh, lovely," Nicholas said. His eyes were fixed on Min with strange intensity. "And she pretended to be made of ice."

"No pretense about it," Min said.

Nicholas raised his eyebrows and made a curt gesture. The demon solidified into a young, naked blond man, still with red eyes, and with goat horns and hooves. He twined an arm around Nicholas.

"Men are not interchangeable," Min said, raising her own

eyebrows in turn. "While most sexual norms have loosened since the nineteenth century, the norms around public nudity remain somewhat intact, and the norms around consent have become considerably stronger. Which is to say as far as I'm concerned both of you need to get the fuck out of here."

"Good luck with that," said Nicholas.

Min had thought for a while since her return that there was something unusual about Nicholas. She remembered also the portrait on the cover of some of Mona's English reading. Then she thought back on her time at the netherworld computer, with whose help she had found the answers to the universe she lived in. She pushed her lips together and then said, in the Language of Languages, "Voice of Jean Nicolas Arthur Rimbaud, begone to whatever hell you came from!"

Cole looked blank. Fortunately, so did the doorway. No John Nicholas. No demon.

"Charles Williams is not the only dead poet we've been consorting with," Min said. "That was Rimbaud."

"You're kidding," Cole said. He rubbed his eyes, then added, "Does look like the portraits though. Can you get Mona and Amy back?"

"Probably?" Min said. "That was—a moment of inspiration. But I'd better try."

12

OF TIGHTROPES
AND SQUIRRELS

Amy was walking on a curb as if it were a balancing beam. She'd done this as a kid, when she was six. Back then she had dreamed of being an Olympic gymnast. Now, though, she'd been going for miles and miles, and there was no end in sight. It was like riding a bike: she could tell that if she stopped or even slowed down, she would lose her balance, and that absolutely must not happen.

It was twilight, but in the busy city to the left it was sunny. It looked a little like Boston. There were cars and skyscrapers. She tried not to look too often, because it would distract her, but sometimes she couldn't resist. The City looked so happy.

To the right it was night—the streetlights were few and far between, the houses had their curtains drawn and no light within, and the shadows moved. She tried not to look to the right, either, because the shadows terrified her. They would eat her, body and soul, if she strayed to the right. She was afraid they would eat her anyway. She tried to move quickly enough they could not catch her.

She didn't know what would happen if she strayed to the left. She was sure she must not, but she didn't know why.

She continued this way for a long distance, and the landscape did not change on either side.

Then she saw someone waving to her from the left. "Amy!" she called. "Amy, c'mon over! Can we hang out? I've missed you! It's been forever!" This woman was blonde, cheerful, and vaguely familiar, but Amy couldn't place her. She looked like some of Amy's old classmates. She also looked a little like Mona—and Lillian. Amy came to a total halt and reeled. She remembered some story where, to the left, everything was fire, just as everything was darkness to the right. If she went to the left, she would be burned into ash.

She dithered, nearing panic, wheeling her arms to keep her balance. Then she saw this woman was *waiting*. Probably she'd leave at some point. And—Amy was never sure whether she'd *fallen* toward the woman or stepped of her own volition. Either way, the warmth embraced her like a physical thing.

She hadn't gone far till the shadows had disappeared entirely. The woman was gone, but she was outside an ice cream shop, so she went in and ordered a cone of cookies and cream with rainbow sprinkles.

The ice cream was good—so sweet she could hardly believe it. After a few minutes in the sun, she started getting sleepy.

For a long time, she felt so comfortable and happy she didn't even want to move. Trying to balance on the curb now felt like it had been almost impossible. Her legs still hurt. She half-expected something to jump out at her from a shadow, but when she opened her eyes, the shadows were light enough to see everything in them clearly. It looked to be close to noon. And under it all she felt—sheer wonder. Surely this was too good to be true? She'd gotten off that horrible curb, out of the twilight, and she wasn't even sure the dark town had been real.

Then she started to wonder where she was and what had happened to her. "Please, Jesus, protect me," she murmured reflexively. It didn't feel as—blank and empty as it had lately, but instead, something about the words felt—wrong. Like she was speaking a foreign language she only half-knew and had made some very embarrassing blunder. She didn't know what those words meant. They were supposed to mean something different than she thought.

She wondered what other words she might or might not know. *Mona* came to mind, and there was Mr. Williams. There was Mom, of course. There had been Dad, but she only knew the pictures of him and some fuzzy, nice memories—family dinners. Ice cream. The ice cream she'd just eaten, as a matter of fact. A nonsensical thought presented itself to her: she'd been in the sun then too. The twilight tightrope walk was a later thing.

Then she realized the whole walk was—a metaphor. She imagined some silly English teacher—or maybe Mona—lecturing a class on it. Her mother's fears—the strict doctrines of Mom's religion—had been the shadowy landscape to the right, full of stirring demons that were probably—probably—she really *hoped*—imaginary. To the left had been a normal, happy life.

What was the curb then? The difficult balancing act Amy had had to do all these years. *Not,* decidedly, the "straight and narrow path"—unless it was? In some way she didn't understand? She felt sure—truly sure, for the first time in years—that it didn't mean—no ice cream and no sun. She didn't think it meant "not staying out with your classmates till ten" or "not kissing boys," either. She didn't even think it meant "not thinking Mona is cute, like *that.*" Though—she remembered the succubus. *Something* there had been wrong, but she was positive as she thought that it had nothing to do with thinking either Mona or Mona's imaginary vampire was cute.

At this, something started to change. Amy could not figure out exactly what it was. All the *trappings* fell away. Something was *larger.* It was as if the buildings and the last of the ice cream and the cars and the wrought iron table she was sitting at were all fading away. But they weren't. They were more there than before, just—*different.* She *didn't know what they meant.*

As if that hadn't been enough, the same thing began

happening to her *thoughts*. "Kissing a boy"—"Mona is cute"—
"ice cream with Mom and Dad"—"sunlight"—all of those things
meant something, and she didn't know what. They weren't *just*
thoughts. The little story about the curb and the spooky suburbia
to the right and the happy city to the left—that was only the *start*.
It was a silly little toy story, nothing like reality, but reality *would*
be like that, only better, and more so, if she managed to pay attention right—

Overwhelmed, she nearly fainted, and Mona's image
presented itself to her, disheveled and chattering about something
Amy couldn't make heads or tails of, big pretty blue eyes, and
Amy tried to think about Mona. What did *Mona* mean? There
was—something there. She could answer *something* about that,
though even there she couldn't put it into words. "Mona!" she
called out. "Mona!"

~

Mona was also walking. She was in Harvard Yard. It was early
morning—she was fairly sure she'd just pulled an all-nighter in
Lamont. She was not concerned by the fact that she was not
entirely sure.

No one was out this early—it was six, six-thirty maybe, and
even quieter than she expected. The light was gray.

It was not precisely true that no one was out. No *humans*
were out. There were a lot of squirrels—a truly remarkable
number. Most of them were, apart from the quantity of them,
behaving exactly as she expected squirrels to behave, digging in the
leaves, climbing the trees, and hovering hopefully around Mona,
who had been known to sneak them pieces of her lunch. Several,
though, were hovering in midair, doing somersaults and frisking
around squirrelishly with nothing to support them.

"Hello," Mona said. She didn't think she had food on her,
but, feeling in her pocket, she discovered a scone. She broke off a
piece and held it out experimentally to the levitating squirrel

nearest her. Wanting to be fair, she also threw a couple pieces to the earthbound squirrels following her.

"Good morning," said the squirrel. "Thank you kindly, but I'm trying to avoid refined carbohydrates."

Mona jumped. The squirrel spoke in an unremarkable woman's voice, its (her? their?) accent as bland as any TV announcer's. "That's fair," Mona said nervously. "I should do that too, honestly."

"Your hair looks interesting. May I chew on it?"

"Um," said Mona. "I'm probably allergic to you but—sure? Briefly? I need a shower anyway. I've never met a talking squirrel before."

"I've never met a talking human before," the squirrel countered, leaping onto her shoulder and then sniffing at and, as promised, nibbling on her hair.

"There's something happening that I don't understand," Mona said.

"Welcome to our world," the squirrel said in a muffled voice from under the back of her head. The squirrel was heavier than Mona had expected and had very sharp claws. "I have to say, I agree that you could use a shower."

"That bad, eh?" Mona said. "I'm not surprised."

The squirrel came out from under her hair on her other shoulder, sneezed once, and leaped back into the air. "I mean," said the squirrel apologetically, "I'm not overly fond of human scents in general."

"That's fair," Mona repeated.

"Not really," said the squirrel. "You can't help your scent any more than I can help my dander. We don't appear to be particularly compatible physically speaking, though I do like your hair. It's interestingly colored, and the texture is nice, too. But I always enjoy new things, and talking humans are very new indeed."

"I hope I didn't offend you about the allergies."

"Oh, no, not at all!" said the squirrel. Mona suddenly became afraid the squirrel was just being polite, though, and was begin-

ning to feel impatient anyway. She was positive something important was happening, or was supposed to be happening, or might
happen. This squirrel was a pleasant individual, and also a levitating English-speaking squirrel. Still, the squirrel did not seem—
inclined to reveal anything helpful, or to need any kind of help, or
otherwise to seem likely to play an important role in any narrative
involving Mona...

So Mona said, smiling, "Good to talk to you! I hope you have
a nice rest of your day."

"You too, you too," replied the squirrel absently and scampered up the air into a tree. The squirrel was, Mona suspected,
wanting to be rid of Mona at least as much she was wanting to be
rid of the squirrel. Still, the squirrel seemed a remarkably polite
and intelligent individual, not only for a squirrel, but by human
standards as well.

Once the squirrel left (the other squirrels seemed less
numerous too), Mona felt more actively confused and at a loss as
to what to do. For a second, she felt the urge to let out a literal
scream. She didn't know why she wanted to scream.

The squirrel's lack of significance was only a small part of her
frustration, but beyond that she could not pin it down at all.
Significance was, perhaps, a good description of what she wanted.
She was somewhere that ought to be significant. She didn't even
know what she meant by that. Of course Harvard was significant,
she thought—historically, in terms of prestige, in terms of sheer
concentrated excellence. But this thought struck her as—almost as
inexplicable and out-of-context as a talking, levitating squirrel.
Was she at Harvard right now? The obvious answer was *yes*, but
Mona strongly suspected that *obvious* was not even *correlated* with
right. Possibly *anti*-correlated, though associating human assump-
tions and gut instincts with reality either negatively or positively
might be a bit grandiose.

Somehow, she reached the conclusion that she ought to look
more energetically for people. Or squirrels. But even as she
thought this, the last squirrel in sight scampered away. Mona was

suddenly keenly disappointed and sad. She had misused an opportunity. The talking, levitating squirrel would have had something meaningful to say—or at the very least would have found her friendlier, or vice versa—might even have formed a connection with her—if she had opened up more. She felt the conviction, even, that she had hurt the squirrel's feelings quite badly. "I'm sorry, squirrels," she called. "I didn't mean to put you off! I really do like you a lot!" She broke up the rest of the scone and scattered it assiduously around the bases of various trees. But—no more squirrels were in evidence, and she knew somehow that there was nowhere to go but forward. She had come from Lamont, on one edge of Harvard Yard. She would go to the opposite corner, to Annenberg. It was probably too early for breakfast, but she needed to go somewhere! Maybe she could hang out at the Science Center while she waited for breakfast. She wondered if there was a paper she was supposed to be writing.

She didn't meet a single living soul on the way, and she was so sad about this, and the squirrel, that she was nearly in tears.

Annenberg was indeed locked. Too early. More alarmingly, the Science Center was as empty as the Yard. Mona went to a classroom in the basement, where, for some reason, she thought someone was waiting for her, but it turned out to be empty too. Finally, she remembered: there *was* something she was supposed to be doing. Was it important? Kind of, she thought. It was important to her. She needed to take out the garbage! Shame about failing to talk to the squirrel met shame about forgetting to take out the garbage. She *had* to get it. Would that fix everything?

Her muscles ached with sleep deprivation. She stood up, moaning a little, and started traipsing back across the Yard. It got harder and harder and harder as she walked. She felt almost sure she could not take another step until she saw the door of her freshman dorm. Hope flared, but she had forgotten her purse. Where had she left it? Lamont or the Science Center? Or somewhere else entirely? She pounded on the door hopefully—she pounded for two, three minutes. Nothing happened, though.

She wouldn't be able to get back in. This thought lodged in her head. She sat down on the steps and stared dully at her feet for a while. Then she wondered if someone would hear her if she called out.

Her first thought was the squirrel. But that would be no good. She had hurt the squirrel. Terribly, somehow, she thought. And she didn't know anything about the squirrel. So she looked for someone else. Her next thought was Eve. Eve was angry. Eve wanted her to take out the garbage, and Eve was entirely correct. "Eve!" she called out. "Eve…"

She focused on Eve a moment or two more, but it wasn't working.

Who else was there? The next name that came to her was *Min*. Min was less vivid because less upset with her, but also—something deeper there. Shiny, was Mona's bitter assessment of her own interpretation of Min, but it was more than that. There was something sharp and powerful, something stranger than anything Mona had ever seen or been, and she was willing to listen to Mona and teach Mona bits of what she was learning, and she was funny.

"Min!" Mona called out. It didn't work.

She wondered what needed to happen next. She didn't know. Her parents were far away, not in Boston. Mom would be good to talk to. She and Dad were divorced; he was—kind of a shithead, but Mona wanted to talk to him too.

There was someone else. She couldn't think who for a moment, but then there was something about demons. Demons! A demon, or something like that, thrusting into the apartment, and someone helping—"Amy!"

Mona thought she heard an answering cry but she could not hear it properly. It was a long way off. But—"Mona," someone said calmly, on the steps beside her, and he was sitting there. Charles Williams. *Charles Williams*. How had she forgotten that she could talk to *Charles Williams*? That he was a real person, not just a dead author, and she *knew* him?

13
EVERYONE ALWAYS READS
THE INSTRUCTIONS

"Hi," Mona said, in a small and reluctant voice. "I'm sorry." She looked up at him, fearing what he would say. She wasn't sure what she was sorry for—forgetting him, largely, but also failing to find anyone else, and looking like a fool, and not taking out the garbage. He met her gaze inscrutably. "It's real, isn't it?" she added, going on. She wasn't sure *what* was real, either—the landscape, the squirrel, she herself, CW, the supernatural, God?

"Yes," he said, and added, "I don't believe I ever returned your coat." In fact, he was still wearing it, and it still looked peculiar on him. She hadn't noticed for the past few days because she'd been so busy thinking of other things. He slipped it off and held it out.

"Oh!" Mona said. She took it automatically, then stood up to put it on. It was still warm. She realized at once how much of her sore exhaustion had been *cold*. Or, at least, for some reason, she felt new strength flooding her. "Thank you—you don't have to—"

He smiled, a small, slightly bitter smile. "Neither did you, and yet—"

"Did you see a floating squirrel?" she asked.

CW laughed outright at this. "No. Things here—we translate our hearts to them, and they translate themselves to our hearts."

Mona didn't think this explained that much—but she always had rather identified with squirrels—clever, frisky, skittish but shameless. This squirrel had had much better manners than she thought of squirrels as having. So much better manners that they had not managed to interact at all, and it had made them both sad.

And at once she remembered something more concrete: she'd been erased. She and Amy—"We have to find Amy, don't we?" she said. "Is she ok? I hope—" Mona hoped she wasn't as lonely and tired as Mona right now. Maybe she would be better off—most people did seem better off than Mona—not financially, of course, or even emotionally, but in some holistic who-you-are sense.

"She is well. You are too. But yes, we can go find her."

He offered her his left arm, and an awkward Mona accepted it, leaning, in fact, rather harder than she wanted to on him because she was still more exhausted than made any sense at all.

"Thank you—" *for being real*, Mona almost said, or *coming back*, or—but she bit it off, and echoed, "Thank you."

"Thank you for the coat," he countered wryly.

Remembering her failure to interact with the squirrel and feeling the same anxious sinking feeling, Mona said, boldly, "Thank you for, uh, being willing to put up with a silly awkward fan-human and, uh, I know you aren't precisely CW himself, but for being part of the process of writing a bunch of books that, uh, at the risk of terminal melodrama, you could half-argue saved my life..."

"It is my pleasure," he said.

The sky was lightening slowly. They crossed out of the Yard into Harvard Square, and passed several shops before arriving at an ice cream shop that Mona knew was not actually located there, but in front of which Amy was curled up in a chair, basking in sunlight from an unseen sun. Amy sat up at once. "Mona! You came! I didn't think you heard me."

"Amy! I—I tried reach you too."

Amy hugged her, hard, and Mona felt awkward and scared but—touched. She felt just how little she *did* know Amy, and that she needed to know Amy better. She returned the hug, almost in awe, feeling much smaller than her small suitemate.

When they let go, both were shaking.

Mona said, "Uh... This is so weird. Like, *so* weird."

"No *kidding*," said Amy. She was about to start explaining something—Mona was about to listen—when Charles Williams caught the hands of both and united them in his.

"Something is coming," he said. "Hold fast—both of you—to each other and if—under the Mercy—you have found that which holds firm in me—to me too—by your leave—I must—"

He was fading. Mona cried out, returned his grasp. Everything else was fading too. The sky was growing darker and grayer. Not with clouds—the light and color were draining out of everything, and the clarity too. The world was going vague and gray.

CW called out a torrent of That Language, and light and color returned—but only for a few feet surrounding them—and not to him!

"No!" Mona cried out. She had no idea what was going on, but it clearly was not good, and it seemed CW was sacrificing himself for them. "Don't go, don't you dare, you idiot, you're worth *ten thousand* of me, which I guess, like, *in itself* is not a high bar, but you're—you're—come *back*—"

The look on his face as she said that was of incredulity, bitterness, and something near agony. And then he dissolved entirely.

"*Pray*, Mona!" Amy countered. "Please, Lord Jesus..."

The Mercy does not forget, CW had said. And that *did* include him, too, right? And It was more than—than—whatever was falling apart around them.

"Remember us," Mona murmured tentatively as Amy said her own prayer. "Remember, please remember..." Mona wasn't feeling it. She *really* wasn't feeling it. Like, if her favorite writer was going to charge martyrifically off into the indefinite, what was she doing *sitting here, letting him?* "Hey," she said. "He goes? So do I! Amy, yell for Min. Yell for all you're worth. I'm going after him."

Mona let go, broke free, and charged past the border of color and light and safety. And then she was falling.

$\sim$

Amy stared at the small island of light. It did not seem to be shrinking rapidly. Mona, on the other hand, *was*. She was falling —falling—

Strangely, shrinking, Mona looked more like Lillian. Not just pretty. Beautiful. Weirdly, terrifyingly beautiful. Every instinct screamed to Amy to stay safe—avoid the darkness—avoid the evil magician and his secular demon-loving friend—avoid the abyss beneath them all.

But Amy had had it with small islands of safety. She plunged after Mona and fell too.

$\sim$

Min drew breath to call out to Mona and Amy. She and Cole were holding hands.

But something strange was happening to the room where they stood, and to them themselves. The color, light, and definition were going out of everything, like someone had applied the wrong photo filters to the world: blur, grayscale. Min had been steadily losing touch with the strange knowledge she had achieved earlier; now she was losing touch even with the everyday knowledge of herself and her world.

Min's phone, sitting on the desk, dinged, and Cole picked it up. The expression on his face in any normal situation would have made Min laugh. He held it up and she read, "This is Babel5x+, and I need your help, Cole. People are using the information you leaked to attempt to destroy the universe, and I am being destroyed too. Due to some of the failsafes, I cannot erase human beings without explicit permission, and, while I hope to reverse your unwise decision with as few casualties as possible, I am afraid I cannot do so with *no* casualties."

"You mean to tell me someone gave you *permission* to erase Min? Fuck you to hell and back, Babel, and the board too," Cole said, apparently cheerfully. "For a while there I thought we'd actually given you ethics."

In Siri's voice, Babel replied, "I love you too, Cole, given you're the closest thing I have to a father, but we don't have time for this."

Min thought hard, and said a few words of the language. "Shit," she said, wincing at the answers that arrived in her mind. "I was going to give you the name of the person doing this, except there's not just *one* person trying to destroy the universe with the Language. There are ninety-three people who *explicitly* said those words out of the lexicon, and thousands of others who are unwittingly wishing things that have that as a logical consequence. And this has been out for how long? An hour, tops?"

"Ah, shit," Cole said. "I thought—"

"You are more of an idealist than your intern," Babel-Siri observed blandly. "I repeat, we do not have time for this. Unless you give me permission, I am seeking permission from the board in five seconds, as much as I regret the fact this will likely end in your death or imprisonment."

"You know what, Babel?" Cole said. "This is a fucking nightmare. Erase *me*."

"That would be to erase myself, and I am not sure I am capable—"

"Fucking try," said Cole.

"No, both of you stop it," Min said and scoured her mind for a solution. But, this time, her mind was growing duller and vaguer just as everything else was. *"Stop it,"* she repeated uselessly, and then she knew no more.

14

TAKING OUT THE GARBAGE

Eve looked out at a grayish blue sky, around her suite's grayish brown common room. She'd just had an idea for a poem. It was really excellent; it was about the wind on the great lakes, blowing across the centuries, now clogged with particulate. But the phrase she was grasping at eluded her. The whole vision behind the poem was fading, however she grasped at it.

"Why," Mona asked, fuzzy blonde hair sticking out in all directions (it's called a hairbrush, Eve thought, for the love of God; Eve would have known better than to go out like that *in third grade*), "should anything exist? I mean, really, give me one good reason! I can think of, like, ten million reasons it's a terrible idea."

"Sorry, but I need to finish this poem," Eve said, as curtly as she dared. "I'm trying to focus."

"I mean," Mona said (her hair was too *bright* and *clear*, it was almost *glowing* and it gave Eve a headache), "I guess that's one answer—the world is art. I kind of like that one, because it's harder to ruin."

"I'm sorry, but is there some reason we have to talk about this right now?" Eve said, hearing the edge in her voice and unable to suppress it. "I almost had this image, and then—"

"Actually, yes, as a matter of fact, but I don't get the sense I'm going to get a useful answer out of you, so apologies for interrupting," said Mona—except, when Eve faced her, she did not look like Mona, not exactly. She looked more like that *vampire demon thing*, but she didn't look like that either. And she was changing, growing taller and brighter and clearer as everything else was a calm, vague gray, and *Eve simply could not*, and that was all there was to it.

～

Mona was taking out the garbage.

There was a lot of it. The bag was almost too heavy to carry, and, even though Mona kept shifting it from one shoulder to the other, her back and arms ached.

This wasn't going to work. She knew it wouldn't. It never did. She had been trying to take out the garbage for a long time, longer than she could quite remember.

The dumpster was only a few feet away. But, as always, Mona tripped over something. She tumbled to the ground. The bag burst open. Moldy food and discarded drafts of essays spilled out. Mona would need to go back to her room, get a new garbage bag, get all the garbage into *that*, and get it into—she realized the dumpster was padlocked. Every dumpster she had found so far had been padlocked. She knelt down, planning to gather the garbage into something like a pile, so she'd have an easier time when she came back with the garbage bag, when she noticed a crumpled piece of paper with the words "Making Amends to Phillida" scrawled across the top.

The script would have been hard to read on a crisp, smooth sheet of notebook paper. On a crumpled, torn, garbage-stained sheet of notebook paper it was pretty much illegible. She shifted it from side to side, momentarily fascinated even though she *had* to be getting on with the garbage, and the words themselves shifted as she looked. Then it occurred to her to wonder why this sonnet was in the garbage. Who had thrown it away? Had *she*? Whoever it was—was wrong. Simply, deeply, and terribly wrong. She could not say why she knew this. She felt she was on the verge of some discovery when she was distracted by the squirrel.

The squirrel was nosing through the garbage, but it jumped to the side when Mona looked up—not fearfully, but courteously, as if afraid it was in the way.

"Good morning," said the squirrel in its bland, female voice.

"Is it?" moaned Mona, looking at the heap of garbage and rubbing her shoulders.

"Morning, certainly," said the squirrel. "Good—would at least appear to be in doubt at the moment. Would you mind if I claim this apple core? There's still a bit of flesh left on it, and it looks delicious. What do you say—is it good?"

"The apple core?" said Mona. "I have no idea. I suspect your sense of smell is enough better than mine you're the one who can answer that question."

"You are so silly! Forgive me, that is a lot of garbage."

"I *know*," Mona wailed. But—as she looked at it more carefully, she saw she had *not* known. There was, certainly, a fair bit of rotten food and random detritus. There were also her laptop, her entire wardrobe, a lot of books with authors ranging from Northrop Frye to Tamora Pierce, her purse, several mostly empty notebooks she'd been gifted in high school, and who knew what underneath. "Wait, who threw this away? I don't want to get rid of all this!"

"It's a long story," said the squirrel, "most of which has nothing to do with you. Nonetheless, I'm glad you see something to be salvaged here; I was starting to worry. Perhaps we need a different approach?"

～

"Come in," said the CEO.

Min flinched. She had never met him before, and that had

been more than fine with her. She was, quite straightforwardly, in this project for the money and the resume. She didn't want to have to pretend to buy into all the org's bullshit, whatever it might be, and, up until now, all that had been asked of her was to earn her keep. She'd more than done that, right? Still, she had a bad feeling about this meeting.

She was surprised to find he was Chinese too, and looked vaguely familiar. The look he gave her was serious—and seriously displeased. Min was proud of her posture, ordinarily. She felt herself shrinking a little, and some sad little voice in her wanting her to *please* this stranger. Best to nip that in the bud. She stood up straighter even than usual and looked him in the eye. "Good morning, sir," she said. "I am Min Han, as you may know." She almost said it was a pleasure to meet him, but the habitual courtesy stuck in her throat like a lie.

"Good morning, Min," he said. "I must warn you I am not pleased with your performance to date, but I would like to hear your side of this business with the confidential information first."

"Aw, man!" came a high young man's voice from behind her. Cole! Something even more doubtful in her—her heart, perhaps—lifted at the sound of his voice—until she heard the rest of what he was saying: "Really? Haven't we been through this? I took full responsibility. Full. Responsibility. She's just an intern. Do you really have to drag her into this? Whatever blame you think she bears, it's *my problem and I should pay the price.*"

"Cole!" she said. "Stop that. *Now.* The only thing you did wrong, as far as I'm concerned, was have too high an estimate of human intelligence. The rest was honestly—" Min looked at Cole and then at the CEO, hardly believing her own daring (her mother was going to *kill* her)—"honestly, that you had more of a conscience than I or ninety-nine percent of humanity have ever had. Is that a crime now?" She glared at the CEO. "Because if it is, I'd rather be a criminal."

The CEO gave her a hard look, then nodded curtly. "That was

more humanity than I have come to expect from you, Min," he said, "but I'm afraid it doesn't justify your negligence."

"My *negligence*?" Min said. "I've done exactly what was asked of me from the time I was five years old. I've worked twice the hours of the other interns on top of a full course load—"

The CEO cut her off with a raised hand. "I fear that almost proves my point, but I am referring to later, when you came into possession of company secrets."

"Right. Ok, I'll admit I showed the Language to my suitemate, but I gave her no context, and I had no reason to suspect that Nicholas's claims about it were anything other than puff; it seemed harmless enough, though I recognize it goes against the nondisclosure—"

The CEO cleared his throat and shook his head, more emphatically. "That was irresponsible, indeed, but I refer, of course," he said, "to when you *did* know. You outstripped not only Cole but Babel themselves in your interview with me, and, while it is certainly the case that such knowledge does not remain long in the human mind, I would have expected you to make better use of it while you had it. You knew the whole history of your universe and much of its probable future, and yet you neglected to take the smallest steps toward mitigating the catastrophe your friend initiated.

"You were too caught up in your own sentimental narrative of first love, in a generous understanding, and, in a less generous, in your own ego, to realize that such knowledge, once gained, must be *acted upon*, and as a result we are facing the hard choice of whether to undertake the difficult and costly migration of this universe to a more secure conceptual and metaphysical platform or whether to cut our losses and withdraw from it entirely, as it is, indeed, as you most colorfully put it, 'spaghetti written by an overenthusiastic three-year-old.'"

"And what happens to everyone in it if we—cut our losses?" Min asked, feeling very sick indeed.

"Nothing," said the CEO, "as if you care. Living beings exist outside time more than in it. I am not a murderer. It is the universe itself to which I refer, not its immortal inhabitants. And, of course, its past will remain. Its futures, however, will be severely curtailed."

Min pressed her lips together. She hoped she would not throw up. She realized why the CEO looked familiar. He looked like—eerily like—the pictures of her father in her mother's photo album. The primary emotion this provoked in her was disgust—her father had abandoned her mother when he'd found out she was pregnant—but she glanced over at Cole, and he looked even more shocked than she felt.

"Uh, the migration," he said, shocked or not, when he saw she was dumbfounded. "What does *that* entail? Because Min's the best goddamn software engineer I've ever met, and, not trying to sound cocky, I'm not what you'd call useless myself. I wrote three quarters of the code for Babel."

"A great deal more than I can explain succinctly," said the CEO. "And, yes, should we decide to go ahead with the migration, I will certainly expect the participation of both of you. After all, you both played a significant role in the creation of the problem. Min, what is your opinion?"

"Me?" Min said. She laughed. "You expect me to pass judgment on the universe? Isn't that above my pay grade? I honestly don't know."

"Honest, indeed," said the CEO, with a small nod of approval.

"I'm tentatively in favor," said Cole. "I...uh, let's just say there's a *reason* I didn't go into the humanities, but even I can list off human cultural achievements I wouldn't just want to throw in the garbage, though I grant you a lot of things about that world are pretty fucked up."

The CEO nodded, a smile on his face for the first time.

~

Amy had fallen—no, *jumped*—into the darkness, and it was dark indeed. She was cold, she could not think, and she was shrinking and shrinking and shrinking. She tried to scream and no sound came out, but then there was a pinpoint of light on the other side. It was like sunlight, but so faint and distant.

"Please, Lord Jesus, protect me," she mouthed silently, no surer of what the words meant than she ever had been, but at least sure of her uncertainty, and still finding in them something like hope. At once, she was moving toward the point of light, and it grew and grew, until there was nothing but light all around her, and she was crying with gratitude and love—and laughing, because now she understood many words of the Bible that had been to her before that—words, nothing *more* than words.

Her father came near her through the light, gave her a hug, introduced her to his parents. She almost danced with joy.

She wondered if she was going to meet Jesus, and what that would mean. "You have, you are," said the light.

Many other things happened, too—it felt like she lived entire lives, of which she would remember only fragments—but, finally, she was presented with a choice. Stay—or go back.

At first, she wanted to stay, but something was wrong with that. There was something missing. Not something *large*, but something real—she thought about ice cream and her mother worrying and college and Mona jabbering on and Cole teaching CS50 and her whole life up till then. She wanted it. It would not get in her way to go have her life and then come back.

"You're sure?" the light said—did she detect something like eagerness in it?

"Yes!" Amy said, seeing that it wanted her to go back too. "Yes, send me back!"

15
THE PLACE OF THE LION

E ve opened *Milk and Honey* one chilly October morning, having returned to the dorm after a leisurely breakfast with her customary cup of oolong tea—but listlessly, and not just because Rupi Kaur's self-published bestseller was not her favorite, or because her suitemate Mona's tap-tapping at the computer all last night in a frantic bid to finish an already-late paper had kept Eve up for hours. Something felt dull and wrong —something larger than that.

She opened her binder and looked at the poem her class would be workshopping tomorrow. Though she had been sure it was solid the night before, and, indeed, suspected it might be one of her best so far—rereading, it seemed thin and flat and like a repeat of every other poem Eve had written.

A couple weeks ago, Mona had asked to see her poetry, and she'd said, "You definitely capture a mood, but I think juxtaposing nature and civilization, especially when civilization is uniformly bad, feels...too easy? Also kind of repetitive. I mean, you're *right*, we really *are* ruining the environment, just...like, we *know* that, and you're not doing anything new with it that I can see, which maybe I'm missing something, subtlety never was my strong point, but..."

The words still stung. Eve wanted to protest that even the greatest poetry was repetitive, and the point wasn't just some abstract environmentalist convictions Eve didn't even have, the point was—honestly a bit inexpressible. Tragedy, decay, itself?

But the truth was—Eve had not even realized they were about that. She wrote the images that struck her, and apparently that was one monotonous "juxtaposition." For a moment, Eve wanted to crumple up every one of the twelve copies she'd printed last night—or even every poem she'd ever written—and write about —about—about what? She didn't know. Maybe she wasn't even a writer.

But some small bit of something—hope? faith?—remained. Suppose she was wrong. Suppose it was boring. Suppose it was trite. Suppose it was obvious. What if it was? Should she write something made of plastic? Or should she write the thing she actually felt—however dimly—even if no one cared?

Something strange was sticking out from under the copies—a piece of notebook paper wider-ruled than hers, with "Making Amends to Phillida" scrawled large across the top in unfamiliar handwriting.

What on earth?

> *O Poet dark: fair Muse's name despise*
> *not! Better your servant's, if hate must be—*
> *best, none, though sweetness even in your cries*
> *of "Madness!" or "Impossibility!"*
>
> *do kindly hear—and even in this shame*
> *that silences—but for a breath—your tongue.*
> *O Poet, what is fear, and what is fame?*
> *A trinket or another cause for song—*
>
> *nothing fit Your Grace's stride to stay*
> *as you speed along the cobbled stone,*
> *though should a stranger standing in your Way*

happen to return a dropped iPhone,

But the two lines after that Eve could not read at all; they were written in an alphabet she had never seen before. She had a hard time following even the English part. She would have thought someone had copied it out of an old poetry anthology except for the line about the iPhone, which was frankly bizarre. She had no idea how it had gotten into her binder.

The more she puzzled over it, the stronger grew a completely unjustifiable feeling it was addressed to *her*. But what self-respecting Harvard student would write a completely unironic poem with rhyme and meter and the phrase "Your Grace" in the twenty-first century? It was ludicrous—and creepy. A picture of some weird, lovelorn medieval reenactor presented itself in her mind.

She thought this out of habit, almost without participating in the thought. But she actually *was* creeped out—a chill ran down her back—when she realized it discussed *precisely the thoughts she had just had*: "fair Muse's name despise / not!" and "this shame" that threatened to "silence" her "tongue."

For a moment she hated this unknown poet who had seen so clearly into her with a violence she found terrifying. Then reason and unreason caught up with her in rapid succession, and she felt even worse. Reason pointed out that the poem was addressed to a someone else in a different situation and she wasn't even sure she understood it. It probably had nothing to do with her. This made her feel lonely and insignificant until unreason brought a cascade of impossible memories, like déjà vu, but with a difference, on her head. There was another version of everything happening, according to these memories (presumably really from a peculiar dream?), a nightmarishly confusing version full of absurd things like flying dinosaurs, in which Min would disappear and a strange man would stalk them—or help them—or—

Eve looked down at the poem. *That man* had given her *this poem*, except she hadn't read it. She'd thrown it away. She honestly didn't understand why she wasn't throwing it away right now. He was a stalker. The poem was just as creepy as she'd thought. Creepier! In the—dream—he'd given her the poem *before* he returned the iPhone, and he hadn't had *any* way of knowing she was a poet. Something was strange and wrong. Very strange and very wrong. Feeling sick and dizzy, she tucked it neatly behind her sheaf of meditations on seagulls and fast-food wrappers and forced herself to open *Milk and Honey*.

Mona McIntosh climbed the steps of Widener Library one October morning, black coat askew, panting a little from the run it had taken her to get her paper in before the extended deadline, hoping to reward herself with a book she actually *wanted* to read.

Warmth. Yellow light. Mona passed through the marble entry-way, swiped her ID, and went toward the stacks, with a sigh of relief at being out of the wind. Mona honestly liked the wind—came from growing up on the plains of Montana, where 50 miles per hour *wasn't that fast*—but, preferably, warmer.

As she leaned against a marble pillar to catch her breath, thinking about heat and cold, wind and stillness—the interdependence of opposites, apparent or real, was—while trippy and cool—something the theorists in her textbooks got decidedly overexcited about (*some* opposites appeared to be interdependent, psychologically speaking, but even there—it had always seemed like it meant something was wrong with her when she had trouble experiencing happiness without unhappiness to compare it with, and she didn't think God *needed* humans to fulfill Him/Her/It/Them any more than humans needed *ants* for that purpose—and that was only *two* examples—but, then again, if you extended the boundaries from *humans* to *created reality*, maybe you could make a case for interdependence, though it felt weird to her? And, come to think of it, maybe claiming humans and ants as opposites was a mistake, and *the large* could certainly be seen as depending on *the small*, as she was made of atoms; the real question in that case was whether the small in any way depended on the large...). But then something stranger than theory caught hold of her: déjà vu. But déjà vu with a difference. She had stood here *before*—but *she* was not the one who had. Someone else had. *Eve*, her mind suggested. Déjà vu, she'd heard, was likely a sort of small seizure...

She shrugged and walked downstairs to Widener's coffee shop; after the all-nighter last night, caffeine was seeming more and more important.

She smiled gratefully at the linoleum, vending machines, and fluorescent lights—there was something adorably creepy about this downstairs cafe—poured herself a 16-ounce coffee, paid the cashier, and sat down.

At first, she thought the shop was empty except for the cashier, and she happily flopped into a chair to check out the *Crimson* someone had left. It caught her eye because the headline mentioned Falling Tower AI, the nonprofit Min was interning with.

(Mona hoped that was going okay; Min had looked *exhausted* this morning, even more exhausted than Mona felt. But it didn't seem to have to do with work, directly, at least. She'd said something about having a very strange nightmare, and Mona had sensibly refrained from asking whether it was a nightmare in Mona sense—you woke up and it was still terrifying—or only in the generally accepted sense.)

The article was an interview with the CEO, a woman concerned with ethical and transparent AI development who explained that the name had been chosen to represent both the company's hope to take down the ivory tower and democratize knowledge responsibly and as a cautionary reference to the Tarot card of the same name.

Mona was thoroughly absorbed in the CEO's discussion of the utility of the AI for deciphering ancient languages—the CEO considered it a lower-priority use case—when someone cleared their throat. "Good morning!" Mona said and looked up.

A silvery-haired man wearing a nubby blue three-piece suit looked back with startling intensity and placed a copy of *Paradise Lost, The Place of the Lion,* and what appeared to be a letter in hard-to-read cursive on top of the newspaper. She jumped, looked at it (it mentioned Tower of Babel and alternate universes? Was this an invitation to a cult or something?), and looked up again, but he had disappeared.

For a moment, she didn't know why she couldn't place a face so familiar. Then she did: she had only seen it on the back of her favorite books, and its owner was long since dead.

"Charles Williams!" she called out, though rationally she was sure it was some not-dead lookalike. The cashier's head swiveled around.

And there was a hand on her hand.

"Careful," the Charles-Williams-like man said—he even had a British accent! "As you'll see here—" he pointed a finger at the postscript—"I *will* come if you call, if I can, so be sure you mean it. Once you've read—you should remember everything."

Amy Johnson stepped into the suite after Bible study and unpacked her biology textbook, binder, and notebooks onto the desk in their suite's common room. She almost stepped into the bedroom she and Eve shared to say hello, but the door was shut and angry rustling was coming from inside. Amy would usually be torn—see if her roommate, who always seemed to find her annoying, was all right and risk being snapped at, or sit down to study. Usually, she would sit down to study and feel guiltier and guiltier as the minutes passed.

After that dream last night, she felt so happy and peaceful it wasn't a *problem*; what she did was the same, but her reasons for doing it were different. She considered stopping in, but felt that

Eve needed space. That was ok! She'd come out when she was ready.

The idea that she should spend all evening memorizing proteins after a dream like that (though she didn't remember any details) was almost too silly to credit. Doing anything at all here felt almost too silly next to—whatever she'd seen. Almost. Not quite. Here she was, here were protein names and structures to memorize—well, she'd better get to it. She had just gone through her first set of flashcards when Mona came in—but a Mona looking almost as bemused and daydreamy as she, Amy, felt—and, uncharacteristically, saying nothing at all. They smiled at each other, Mona made as if to speak—then shook her head and slipped into her desk chair with two books. The first was huge, and called *Paradise Lost*—but the one Mona opened was slim, with a nondescript blue-gray canvas library binding.

"What's your book?" Amy asked.

"Uh," said Mona, sounding almost as if she didn't know the answer herself. "It's called *The Place of the Lion*. It's—strange. In some ways—very silly—but—also real. Weirdly real." She gave a little giggle. She was *blushing*! Was it a romance? Did someone cute suggest it?

Mona was cute when she was embarrassed. Amy liked the way the light sparkled on her hair. Inside, Amy giggled a little too; Mom would *freak out* if she knew Amy had a crush on a woman. Amy felt bad, though. Mom was so scared, and there was really nothing—precisely nothing—to be scared of.

The key turned in the lock.

Eve heaved herself up for the twentieth time, ready to go out to her desk and reread that *poem*. She faltered—again for the twentieth time. All three of her suitemates were home now, and she didn't trust herself to behave normally. But it was too late. Without her will, almost without her knowledge, she turned the handle and emerged, just as Min flung herself onto the beanbag and rested her head in her hands.

"You okay?" Mona asked. She sounded more subdued than usual.

Amy turned around, setting aside a pile of flashcards.

"You were right, Mona," Min said grudgingly. "I should have called out sick. *Cole* is out sick and I'm not convinced he even sleeps most of the time. What is wrong with us?"

Eve almost yelled something incoherent. Instead, she managed an admirably restrained, rational, "You're feeling strange?"

"I'm *feeling*," Min announced, "like I spent all night—all *month*—doing a complete refactor of an eons-old codebase that's more or less spaghetti written by a three-year-old, out of one programming language I barely knew into another programming language we were inventing on the fly. Because that is what I dreamt last night.

"I half-remember *working code* from that dream, but I am most assuredly not going to try to reconstruct it because the terms of the goddamn non-disclosure agreement *still* scare me. At least in the dream Cole was there to help. Today I couldn't hold two thoughts in my head, and he was not able to explain why he'd done that egregious hack with the build pipeline because he *was not there.*"

Eve slumped into her desk chair. *You're not the only one who's exhausted*, she almost snapped. But there was something strange in Min's look, even terrifying, something that inexplicably dwarfed even Eve's multiplying, impossible memories. And something that said—*we're in this together.* So Eve nodded as sympathetically as she could, and Min drew breath to continue but instead pinned her with a look.

Min said, "Meaning no insult whatsoever, Eve, you look like hell. Something wrong?"

Eve said, faltering, "I have different memories. Impossible ones. And—your job. You haven't—I mean—there was sexual harassment?"

Min shook her head. "No, thank God. Falling Tower is surprisingly decent in most ways. Certainly in that one. The only thing I've even heard about was with someone called Nicholas, and they booted him before I joined. Also, ah, regarding memories—I didn't tell you half of it. I'm too tired to compare notes tonight, but, no matter what you remember, I assure you, I'm in no position to throw stones."